Unsung Hero

Love never dies...

Judy Kentrus

Unsung Hero

Copyright 2022 by Judy Kentrus

All rights reserved. No part of this publication may be reproduced, distributed, or transmitted in any form or by any means, including photocopying, recording, or other electronic or mechanical methods, without the prior written permission of the publishers, except in the case of brief quotations embodied in critical reviews and certain other noncommercial uses permitted by copyright law.

Author: Judy Kentrus

www.judykentrus.com

Publishers Note: This e-book of fiction was written for your own personal enjoyment. Names, characters, places, and incidents are a product of the author's imagination. Any resemblance to actual events or locales or persons living, or dead is entirely coincidental. No part of this book may be reproduced or transmitted in any form or by any means, electronic or mechanical, including photocopying, recording without the permission in writing from the publisher.

Book Title: Unsung Hero

Edited by: Joyce Lamb Editing

Dedication

This book is dedicated to

Sergeant James Berweiler, Ret.,

a true hero, who served his country in the

U.S. Air Force in Vietnam.

~ 5 ~

What is a hero?

A warrior who shows a great deal of courage, conviction, and risks their lives to help others.

Shane Wallace never considered himself a "hero."
He loved his country and served honorably in the U.S. Navy, retiring six month ago. His life is in a holding pattern, waiting to figure out which direction to take.

His best buddy asks him to be a groomsman in his wedding. Shane and his German Shepherd, Liberty, stay in a campground close to Mt. Rushmore, South Dakota, one of the most patriotic locations in the United States, the first week in July.

When a cat from the neighboring campsite takes off after a squirrel, Liberty joins the free-for-all. The owner is beside herself with worry when the cat runs up a tree. Shane volunteers to save her pet. Unknowingly, the cat is a celebrity and the feline's fans gathered to witness her rescue. Shane flinched when they called him a hero and reluctantly held back claiming, I'm no such thing.

Taylor Parish spends ten months of the year teaching history to middle school children. She spends the rest of her time, driving a converted school bus, nicknamed

Tillie. Her co-pilot, is a striped Toyger cat, named Winnemucca.

With the campground being in close proximity to Mt. Rushmore in the Black Hills of South Dakota, she's looking forward to doing research for the next book in her, YA series, *Adventures with Tillie.*

She didn't count on her mischievous cat needing to be rescued by her neighbor. She wrote about men and women of courage in her books, but this was the first time she'd met one in real life. Puzzled by his strong aversion to the word hero, she decides to make Shane Wallace understand the true meaning of the word "hero."

~ 7 ~

Unsung Hero

Chapter 1

"Winnie, we're here. Hold on to your ears. One, two, three."

Bang! A black cloud shot out from the bus's tail pipe and took to the air. Taylor had gotten so used to the signature backfire from her classic bus she no longer jumped. She used the tips of her fingers to give the dashboard gentle pats. "Thanks for getting us here, old girl."

She shifted around in the driver's seat to see her bestie licking her paws. "I really need to start talking to humans." When she moved to stand up, the creak from seasoned leather was another signal they'd reached the end of their journey. She stretched her arms wide. She'd been driving for nine hours with only a stop for gas and a potty break.

"Let's get the utilities hooked up."

Of course, there wasn't a response, but the saucy feline jumped up on the back of the couch and looked out the window. Taylor opened the door and enjoyed her first breath of warm South Dakota air. The campground was full. On one side of her was a late-model Class C motor home. On the other was a pickup pulling a toy hauler. She'd always been intrigued by that type of RV and wondered what the owner carried in the expanded back end of the trailer.

Many eyes were drawn to her mint-green converted school bus, nicknamed Tillie, especially the cartoon painted on the side of a yellow-and-green-striped school bus being driven by a redheaded woman wearing a WWII leather flying helmet and oversize goggles. Her co-pilot was a striped Toyger cat wearing the same style hat and goggles. Adults scratched their heads, wondering who defied convention by driving such an attention-grabbing vehicle. The reactions of middle-school children were the total opposite.

Having kids knock at her door to ask about Tillie and Winnie was a given. When she'd made the reservation, she'd let the owner know she'd love to have a Reading With Tillie night at one of the nightly campfires. No story time would be complete without her aunt's mascot, Winnie, making an appearance. Her gold, black and white stripes portrayed her as a miniature tiger.

With the campground being in close proximity to Mount Rushmore in the Black Hills of South Dakota, she'd had to make the reservation at one of America's popular national parks six months ago.

Routine came easily—hooking up the water, electricity, and septic. No matter how many times she'd done this, she made sure she chose the white hose for the waterline. She'd even remembered to carry a wrench to tighten the hose connection at the faucet, not wanting to waste natural resources.

She stepped inside and turned on the air conditioning. A few knocks in the older system were a reminder the unit would have to be replaced. She stood under the vent and lifted her face to let the chilled air cool her heated skin. She helped herself to a bottle of water from the full-size refrigerator, making a note to add bottled water to her shopping list.

The living room area was the first thing visitors saw when they stepped inside the motor home. The navy couch opened to a full-size bed. Red and gold pillows added color to the dark fabric. Navy-and-white-striped curtains on the small windows were tied back to let in the natural light.

The long, narrow bookshelf and rolltop desk had been a thrift-store find she'd refurbished. Visitors were also surprised to see the shiny silver stack on her small woodstove.

She'd barely taken a seat at her writing desk when Winnie sprawled across the top shelf. "I'm not ignoring you. This is a momentous occasion." Taylor retrieved the aged journal from the top drawer. Before opening the book, she traced her finger over the initials carved into the leather. TP. Aunt Tillie had showered Taylor with lots and lots of love, becoming both mother and father to a brokenhearted five-year-old after her parents were killed in a plane crash.

"Aunt Tillie, I miss you so much, but knowing I've been able to follow in your footsteps and fulfill your dream makes me feel close to you."

~ 10 ~

She opened the book to the list of places her aunt had put together twelve years go. With her dream of touring the country in a converted school bus, the book series *Touring With Tillie* had been born. The retired schoolteacher had been able to complete only six books before she'd passed away four years ago.

Taylor put a checkmark next to Mount Rushmore National Memorial. Needing to share her happiness at checking off another location on her aunt's bucket list, she picked up Winnie and swung the cat around before gathering her close for a loving hug. "She'd be proud of us!"

The cat's response was a smooth meow.

"Now, let's see what we have for our dinner. Tonight, we relax, and tomorrow I pick up my rental car so I can start exploring the area."

The cat focused her attention on something out the window and swished her long, tiger-striped tail. Taylor just shook her head, watching a squirrel dart across the grassy area that bordered the campsite. "Leave the squirrels alone!"

Taylor turned on the water faucet by the kitchen sink to wash her hands, and nothing came out. "Great. Now what? I know I hooked up everything right." A moment later, she realized what she hadn't done. "You'd get water if you turned it on."

She walked outside and hurried over to the brass nozzle, gave it a few turns, and the white hose wiggled around like a snake to indicate the water was flowing through it. A darting movement to her right

~ 11 ~

had her turning quickly to see her cat chasing a squirrel.

"Dang! Winnemucca! Get back here!" She took off running.

*****

"My baby! My baby! Mama, she's drowning!"
Bang!

Shane jerked awake at the startling noise, and his eyes flared open. "What the heck was that?"

He attempted to sit up, but the pressure on his chest was so great, he couldn't move. He blinked a couple of times, coming face-to-face with a long snout and black nose.

"Liberty, you're no lightweight!"

Undaunted by her master's reference she might be overweight, the German shepherd kissed Shane on the cheek with her tongue.

"My shouting scared me, too. Sorry if I frightened you. The dream gets more real every time." The bed shook slightly when Liberty jumped off the queen-size mattress. Shane swung his legs over the side and scrubbed his hands over his cheeks. The rough surface of his cheeks scratched his palms. Time to shave off his three-day-old beard that had started to itch.

The time on his watch read four-thirty. "What forty-two-year-old guy takes a long nap in the middle of the afternoon?" One who was still feeling the effects of his best friend's bachelor party and wedding three

~ 12 ~

days ago. It was Benny's second time at the altar, but Shane wished the couple all the best. Getting together with six of their other friends had also offered the opportunity to reminisce about college days. Except for Shane, they were all happily married with children. They hadn't missed the opportunity to tease him about avoiding what they'd called the old ball and chain. His excuse? He hadn't found a woman who could make him laugh.

He looked out the small bedroom window. Three hours ago, the space next to his trailer had been vacant, but he'd gotten a neighbor since then. From the proximity of the loud bang, it had come from… He paused, blinked a few times to make sure he wasn't hallucinating. It wasn't every day you saw a vintage school bus painted mint green. A clever hand had painted a redhead behind the wheel of a striped school bus. A black-and-gold-striped cat was hanging out a side window. Both wore WWII leather flying helmets and oversize goggles. *Adventures with Tillie* was scrolled above the humorous logo.

"If the driver of that bus resembles the drawing, we need to keep our distance."

Liberty ran toward the side door of the trailer and wagged her tail.

"You want to go out?"

"Woof!"

"Let me get my shoes and your leash."

The tail stopped wagging at the mention of the word *leash*. "If we were boondocking in a remote area, I could let you go, but it's not possible in the campground. If you play nice with the other dogs in the doggy area, I'll make you a burger."

The tail resumed wagging, this time a lot faster.

"Sometimes, I think you do that just so I'll make you people food."

Shane had barely taken three steps away from his trailer when a woman dashed past him, calling out the name Winnemucca. Who in their right mind would name their kid Winnemucca? Liberty wasn't one to calmly accept a freewheeling person running past her and tugged hard on the leash.

His grip on the leather strap wasn't strong enough. He, too, took off after his dog, who ran after the woman, who ran after someone named Winnemucca. If he weren't so worried about his dog getting lost in the sprawling campground, he'd find the situation comical.

The mysterious Winnemucca apparently had headed for the forest that surrounded the campground. A thick coating of dried pine needles and pinecones covered the dirt, creating an uneven surface for running.

The woman with the long legs, showed off nicely in black denim shorts paired with a red sleeveless tank, was easy to follow. He'd narrowed the distance between them, but Liberty surpassed the woman and stopped at the base of a pine tree. Liberty put her front paws on the trunk and barked.

Shane bent over and took a few deep breaths before grabbing the leather loop. "Liberty! Enough!"

~ 14 ~

When she didn't stop barking, he issued a command that had been given to him by the dog's previous owner. "By my side." The German shepherd immediately quieted down and moved to sit beside Shane.

The woman had a free-flowing shawl of dark brown hair that swept her back. How she'd been able to run in thong flip-flops, he'd never know. Her hands gripped one of the lower branches of the tree, but her eyes were focused on the thick branches overhead.

"Winnemucca, leave the squirrels alone!"

"Lady, can you please tell me who or what is up in that tree?"

"My cat," she quickly replied, but refocused her attention on the feline in the tree.

"What's a Winnemucca?"

"She's a Toyger breed and is named after Sarah Winnemucca, a Native American born in 1844." The rattled woman stepped back and threw her arms wide. "Why am I explaining the significance of my cat's name when I should be trying to figure out how I'm going to get her down?"

"Since she climbed up there, she should know how to get down."

The woman shook her head. "It's not that simple. Winnie has no problem climbing trees to go after squirrels, but she has a problem getting down. The only thing I can do is go to the front desk. Maybe they can call someone with a cherry-picker truck."

Don't do this, his conscience warned, but he had nothing better to do. He held out Liberty's leash.

~ 15 ~

"You hold on to Liberty. She's also got a thing about chasing squirrels. Will your cat come with me if I go up there to get her?"

Shocked at his offer, she asked, wide-eyed, "You'd really climb the tree to save my cat? You're a true hero!"

Hero. He immediately flinched. The word was a sore spot in his vocabulary. *I'm no such thing.*

"Just being a Good Samaritan. Will she try to scratch my eyes out?"

She put the flat of her hand over her heart. "Oh, no. Winnie is a sweetheart, but she's scared and will go with you."

The lower branches offered enough footing for him to start climbing the tree. Prickly points from the pine needles attacked his exposed skin. He made the mistake of looking up to get a location for the adventurous cat and was stabbed in the cheek by a cluster of pinecones. The squirrel was long gone. Winnie had made herself comfortable on one of the thicker branches close to the tree trunk. Her long, tiger-striped tail swung back and forth, like she didn't have a care in the world. The striped tail reminded him of something, but he couldn't place what.

Two branches higher, and he came face-to-face with said cat. "Winnie, you don't look the least bit frightened. It's time to return to your mother."

He lifted the cat from the tree branch, and she gave no resistance when he secured her in the bend of his arm. He'd like to think the meow Winnie gave him was her way of saying *thank you.*

~ 16 ~

Descending was more of a challenge, as he could use only one hand to grasp the rough bark. He looked down to gauge the distance to the bottom branch, but was greeted by a big smile on Winnie's owner's face. Flecks of gold sparkled in her big brown eyes. She'd climbed up onto the first two branches and was reaching up to take the cat from his arms.

"Winnemucca! No more running after squirrels!" The chastisement was followed by a bunch of kisses to the feline's head, which was rewarded with purring.

Shane jumped down to land on a bed of dried pines needles and received a round of applause. In the time it had taken him to climb the tree, curiosity had drawn a number of fellow campers. Momentary panic set in when he realized the woman was no longer holding Liberty's leash.

Shane saw that Burt, the man who had checked him in at the front desk, had arrived in one of the many golf carts that were used to get around the campground. Safely secured in his hand was the end of Liberty's leash.

The guests gathered around the mischievous cat and took turns giving her soothing pats.

"We're so excited to see Winnemucca in person. Will she be okay to appear at your reading?" The woman who'd asked was holding the hand of a young boy who continued to pet the rescued cat, who appeared to be enjoying the attention.

"She's fine," the cat owner assured.

~ 17 ~

Shane retrieved Liberty from Burt and stepped back. *What's so special about that darn cat?*

"Come on, Liberty, let's head back to the trailer. I smell like I've been doused with an entire can of pine forest room deodorizer and need to take a shower."

They'd covered half the distance back to his campsite when hurried footsteps behind him made him turn around to see Winnemucca safely cuddled in her owner's arms. He paused so the woman could catch up to him.

"Wait! I want to thank you. Winnie draws a crowd wherever we go. Are you okay?" She kept a safe distance from the dog, who sat beside him. "Is Liberty okay with cats?"

He didn't think it appropriate he discuss his need for a shower. "She's comfortable with all animals except squirrels and chipmunks." The woman really did have beautiful eyes.

"I don't know how to thank you."

"Would it be too much to ask your name?"

"With all the craziness, that was rude of me not to introduce myself." She kept one arm around the cat and held out her hand. "Taylor Parish."

"Shane Walker." The strength of her hand in his confirmed she really was glad to meet him. His grandfather had taught him at an early age you could judge a person's character by their grip when you shook hands. They were either being polite or were genuinely sincere in their greeting. Taylor Parish was very sincere.

~ 18 ~

"On vacation?" she asked when they started walking again.

"Something like that." He wasn't about to tell a total stranger his life was in a holding pattern, and he was waiting to figure out which direction to take. How many other men retired at forty-two had no obligations other than taking care of his dog and making sure the gas tank of his truck was filled?

When she stopped beside the mint-green bus, his interest in his lovely neighbor went a whole lot deeper. In his travels around the country, he'd never seen a converted school bus. His mechanical brain generated a lot of questions.

His eyes shifted from the comedic character painted on the side panel as he made the connection with the cat's striped tale. "Winnemucca is the cat on the bus, but you definitely don't resemble the wild-eyed bus driver." *You're a heck of a lot prettier.* "How do you fit into all of this?"

Chapter 2

How did she fit into all of this? It wouldn't make much sense to come out with, *Once upon a time...* Though she wouldn't mind sharing the long story with her very handsome hero. When she came face-to-face with readers of *Adventures with Tillie*, middle schoolers expected to see the eccentric, wild-haired redheaded woman painted on the bus. That had been Aunt Tillie, right down to the red hair.

Winnie wiggled in her arms. Taylor tightened her hold. Opportunities to spend time with a good-looking guy were rare, especially one she figured was close to her own age. The ring finger on his left hand was bare, with no *I just removed it to pick up a woman* tan line. Right now, she couldn't appear less attractive. Her flyaway hair was a tangled mess. The dangling ends of her frayed denim shorts tickled her knees. The face of Fonzie from *Happy Days* on her T-shirt had faded from too many washings. *He's definitely a handsome prince, but you're camping, not dressed like Cinderella to go to a ball.*

Taylor decided to do something she practically never did—go out of her way to become friends with someone from the opposite sex. Her married friends at school had set her up on blind dates, but those men's personalities had gone with hers like oil and water.

Shane Walker had proven to be kind, thoughtful and heroic. With the untidy length of his

~ 20 ~

deep-brown hair and scruffy beard, he had a rough-around-the-edges look she favored, rather than the look of a Wall Street trader who sat behind a desk all day.

The dried blood on his cheek caught her attention. She ran the tip of her finger down his cheek.

"Your hero wound needs a bit of first aid. I'm not a Nurse Nancy, but I've got a complete first aid kit."

He ran a finger over the gouge in his cheek. "Hero wound," he repeated with a smirk. "I had a go-round with a bunch of pinecones. I'll put some antiseptic on it when I get back to the trailer."

This was the second time she'd called him a hero, but he seemed to have an aversion to the word. Why? "I'd like to thank you for saving Winnie. I'm making burgers, fries, and grilled veggies for dinner if you'd like to join me. Unless you have plans with your family," she quickly added. She needed to confirm he didn't have a significant other.

"No family. It's just me and Liberty. As for your invitation, my food supply is pretty thin, so I'll take you up on your invite. I can assure you I'm not a convicted felon."

"Neither am I," she teased right back. "Come over at six-thirty."

Taylor bent to one knee and patted Liberty on the head. "Thank you for your help. You're welcome to join us, too."

"See you later," he said, tugging on the dog's leash. "I hope your dinner invitation comes with an explanation as to how you fit into all this," he added, gesturing to the images on her bus.

He really is interested in me. "I can assure you it won't be boring."

She stepped inside the bus and set Winnie on the couch. "I should be giving you a lecture for running out, but I'm at fault, too. I didn't close the door all the way. This time, everything worked in my favor." The cat was undaunted by the lecture and licked her paws.

"If you could talk, you'd tell me I was crazy to invite a perfect stranger to dinner." When he'd given her his name, she'd thought it sounded familiar. Aunt Tillie had teasingly called her Curious Taylor, like the fictional Curious George, when she'd been a kid.

The Internet had become her best friend. She had a few minutes before she had to prep dinner. She opened her laptop and Googled his name. A dozen articles appeared about a Navy diver who'd saved a family and two of his fellow divers during a rescue operation after a tsunami in Japan. He'd also saved the beloved baby doll of the young girl he'd pulled from the water. The heroic rescue had made national headlines. The Navy diver's name was Dane Walker.

Further searching revealed a photo of Shane, Dane, their admiral father, and their grandfather, who was a Navy chaplain, at a ceremony honoring the Walker family at the US Naval Academy in Annapolis, Maryland.

The butterflies in her stomach went a little crazy. Her dinner guest was breathtakingly handsome

~ 22 ~

in the photos in full dress Navy whites. "You're a handsome devil, Shane Walker, and you just confirmed you're not a serial killer."

So many questions had been raised, though. When she'd asked if he was on vacation, he'd replied only, "Something like that."

The name of his German shepherd was unique. Liberty. Was she trained in search and rescue?

"Taylor, take a step back. You don't come right out and pump him for personal information. Let him do the talking."

Time was passing, and she had to start dinner. Taylor washed her hands at the sink before taking a package of ground beef from the refrigerator. Normally, she'd make four patties and freeze three for future meals, but tonight she'd be grilling all four. Her fingers stilled after she'd covered the patties with clear wrap. When was the last time she'd invited someone to have dinner with her on the bus?

Shane would be the first. No, she wasn't antisocial. She had lots of friends, her students, and coworkers. She was captain of a bowling team. She sang in a church choir.

Winnemucca was her only traveling companion, though, along with her computer. That was really sad.

She sliced up a tomato, washed a few pieces of lettuce and put them on a paper plate in the refrigerator. Hopefully, he liked roasted fresh asparagus and broccoli. She'd just finished cleaning up

~ 23 ~

when she realized she didn't have dessert. "What kind of hostess am I? I can't even offer him sweet treat!"

The feline jumped up on the counter and flicked her tail toward the bowl of apples Taylor had purchased two days ago at a farm stand. It wasn't the first time the cat had read her mind.

"You want me to make an apple pie? That's a great idea, but I don't have time." Then she remembered the crescent roll dough in the refrigerator. "Winnemucca, I'm no Betty Crocker, but I can make something that will be close to apple pie. Plus, I have vanilla ice cream."

Winnie earned a kiss on the head.

The quick and easy turnovers came out perfect. The lingering scent of cinnamon gave the interior of the bus a pleasant aroma.

The time on the microwave above the gas stove read 5:30 p.m. That gave her all of an hour to take a shower and make herself appear a lot more feminine. Her summer wardrobe was sparse, but she had one outfit that would be perfect. She was really looking forward to spending time with Lieutenant Shane Walker.

*****

The water pressure in the campground was pretty decent. Shane held his head under the full spray a little longer, making sure the pine smell was gone. He'd purposely increased the size of the holding tank when he'd purchased the used toy hauler six months

~ 24 ~

ago. He blinked away the sting of the shampoo that ran into his eyes.

He used his last clean bath towel to dry off. The clean-shaven face staring back at him in the mirror over the sink took some getting used to, considering he still had to use a comb to manage his longer hair. Like the beard, it had become annoying. The scratch from his encounter with the pinecones was hardly visible now that he'd washed away the blood.

He put the bath towel in his overflowing hamper. His to-do list was getting longer. Get a haircut, buy food, do laundry, replace the propane tank on the barbecue grill. When had he become so neglectful of taking care of his basic needs?

No-brainer there. He'd spent the past six months traveling around the country, living the life of a carefree vagabond. Alone, but for his dog. That didn't say very much for a guy who had no problem enjoying female company. The adage *women were attracted to a man in uniform* never got tiresome. He'd been living proof. These days, the only female who shared his bed snored like a drunken sailor.

His late grandfather had been a Navy chaplain, so Shane had learned about the Bible at an early age. He remembered a saying from the book of Genesis: *It is not good for the man to be alone. I will make for him a suitable helper.* He just hadn't found the right "helper."

Liberty had made herself comfortable on the queen-size bed when he'd stepped into the bedroom. The thumping sound from her tail hitting the mattress

~ 25 ~

let him know she was happy to see him. He sat down next to her and swept her head with a gentle hand.

"As much as I love you, dog, I need to communicate with humans. On the plus side, Taylor is very easy on the eyes. You'll be okay alone for a couple of hours." Now that he'd retired, they were always together. The dog would wait in the truck when Shane went into a store.

He opened the closet, searching for something other than a T-shirt and a pair of cargo shorts. Half the space was taken up by white dress shirts, navy trousers and a formal uniform jacket. Two pairs of black dress shoes that bore a mirrored shine sat on the floor.

"You've walked away from that life, so why are you holding on to all of this stuff?"

Because tradition was ingrained in your life since the day you were born!

There wasn't time to think about why he couldn't let go of his past. Spending the evening with the lovely Taylor Parish would be exactly what he needed to pull him out of his slump.

He found a green-and-white-windowpane-check shirt with not too many wrinkles and paired it with beige chinos. He opened the cabinet in the bathroom to see if there was anything that might resemble aftershave. None was to be found. *Add to shopping list.*

He was retrieving his sneakers from the side of the bed when his cell phone rang. Caller ID showed his father's name. He'd go for months without hearing from his father or brother, but this was the third call in two days. He'd ignored them both. They wouldn't stop, so he decided to face the situation.

"Hi, Dad."

"About time you took my call! I saw your brother yesterday. He said he saw you at the wedding. All the men were in their dress whites but you!"

"I'm no longer in the Navy."

"And that's another thing. When are you going to come to your senses? I can have you reinstated at full rank."

His gut tightened every time he had this conversation with his father, a conversation that always ended the same way. "Dad, retired military personal can only be recalled during times of war, national emergency or 'needs of service.'"

"I'm not talking about a recall. You can be reinstated with a military retainer fee. I can have you recalled to active duty anytime the service wants you."

He ran his fingers through his hair, the hair he'd just neatly combed. "Dad, I chose to retire, so don't do me any favors having me recalled or reinstated with a military retainer fee."

He wanted to say, *You've thrown military life at my feet from the time I could walk. Now it's my turn to walk in the direction I want to go.* He just hadn't decided which direction that might be, though he wasn't about to tell his father that.

"I know why you retired. You can no longer face living in the shadow of your brother's hero status. Being a hero isn't in all of us, but it takes something

~ 27 ~

extra in a person to put the needs of others above their own safety. Your brother is that kind of person."

Slam dunk! Hole in one! Right in his gut. Shane was a coward, and his brother was a hero. *Let's toss a little more mud on my reputation. Today, I saved a cat! That should count for something.*

His father continued to rattle in Shane's ear. "You're part of a military family, so you can be proud of that. I can get the paperwork started as soon as we're done talking."

He was so done with this conversation and needed to end it before he said something he might regret. "Dad, you're the one who's done all the talking. I'm happy, so let's leave it at that."

"This discussion is far from over. Where are you?"

"Mount Rushmore. I'll be here for the rest of the week."

His father's laughter filled Shane's ear. "At lease you'll be able to celebrate the Fourth of July surrounded by heroes!"

Nothing like having his good mood shattered by a phone call. After hanging up, he drew in a deep breath and shoved his fingers through the hair that had fallen across his forehead.

"Liberty, do I look presentable?"

Three hard thumps on the mattress was her reply.

"I'm not nervous," Shane muttered just before he knocked on the door to her bus. Taylor opened the door, and he suffered his second slam dunk in the gut

~ 28 ~

of the evening. The woman who'd climbed into a pine tree to get her cat had transitioned from pretty to beautiful. The smile and lovely eyes were the same.

She embodied the word *feminine* in a strapless sundress the color of pink corral he'd seen in the South Seas. Dark wavy hair swept her naked shoulders. Her skin was a golden tan, an obvious sign she'd spent some time in the sun. He curled his fingers, eliminating the urge to brush his finger over the choker of small pink seashells around her neck. He swallowed hard once, twice, three times.

"Right on time." She walked back up the two stairs to let him in. Once again, she was wearing flip-flops.

Whatever he'd expected the inside of a converted school bus to look like didn't come close to what he was seeing now. Nickle-gray wood-grain panels covered the arched ceiling. The living room had two couches with colorful pillows. A beautiful antique desk created the perfect writing space. Custom bookcases with glass doors housed a small library of books in the space between the windows and ceiling.

Spending hours enjoying a book had become part of his new routine. He was tempted to look over the spines, but he didn't want to appear nosy. Hopefully, he could do that next time.

Privacy curtains separated the living room from the bedroom. Old-fashioned brass-framed lamps with shades were attached to the walls. His eyes widened at the raised platform that supported a small woodstove backed by a red-brick wall. It was all so amazing.

~ 29 ~

"I can tell by the wide-eyed look on your face you're overwhelmed."

Shane gave her a sheepish smile. "Sorry to be so obtuse, but this is the first time I've ever been in a refurbished school bus. This is impressive."

She swept a hand around the interior. "That she is. The mechanic told me she's got a 3800 T444E Navistar International engine, one of the older models. The company changed the design after 1979. No matter how many mechanics have looked at it, they tell me, 'Tillie is an old soul,' and I should pray on her every night."

"Did you have this remodeled yourself?"

"No, it belonged to my aunt, Tillie Payne. My parents were killed in a plane crash when I was five. My mother's sister, Tilda, became my guardian. She left the bus to me when she passed away four years ago."

The watery film that covered Taylor's brown eyes let him know how hard it was for her to talk about the woman who'd raised her. Winnie came over and brushed against her mistress's ankle.

Shane quickly changed the subject. "Is the troublemaker okay? I left Liberty at home." He kept it to himself the animals should get to know each other slowly. Hopefully, they'd be spending more time together.

"She's fine. I'll give you the rest of the tour, and then I'll put the hamburgers on. The vegetables are already grilling."

~ 30 ~

She leaned in close, drew in a small breath and smiled. "Shane, don't take this the wrong way, but you clean up nicely. The pine smell is gone."

He did something he hadn't done in a long time. He burst out laughing.

Chapter 3

From the scent of grilling meat coming from all directions, their fellow campers had taken advantage of the mild evening to cook outside.

"The burgers tasted so much better tonight. Not because I made them, but it has to be the company," Taylor said before wiping her mouth with a paper napkin. Anticipating her guest would eat two hamburgers had been a smart move. Wanting to make things a little more festive, she'd covered the picnic table at her campsite with a red-and-white-checkered tablecloth. It showed off the red, white, and blue paper plates and napkins she'd purchased at the Dollar Store.

"I'm not fond of vegetables, but broccoli and asparagus never tasted so good. I can grill a decent burger or steak. Since it's just me, I go with anything fast, right down to frozen dinners in the microwave." He drank some of the iced tea in his red plastic cup. "This has been very nice, right down to the Fourth of July napkins."

Manners demanded she didn't cringe on his unhealthy eating habits. "Those who know me are aware I'm a holiday junkie and have napkins for just about any kind of celebration. I spend the entire summer on my bus, so I try to keep my living arrangements as normal as possible, right down to cooking healthy."

~ 32 ~

Giggles behind her had Taylor turning her head. Two tweens standing there were clutching *Adventures with Tillie* graphic novels. She remembered seeing the kids this afternoon when Winnie had been rescued. The young boy and girl wore souvenir T-shirts from Mount Rushmore. Their sun-burned cheeks were a sign they'd spent time in the sun.

Taylor swung her legs over the bench and stood up, adding a smile. "Hi! What are your names?"

"I'm Luca, and this is my sister Serenity."

"It's nice to meet both of you. Do your parents know you're here?"

"We're staying in the cabins over there," he said, pointing to the log cabins. "That's my mom sitting on the porch. She's feeding our baby sister."

Taylor searched out the cabin he was pointing to and waved to their mother.

"We were at the rescue today. Is Winnemucca okay?" Luca asked. "We've read all the books. Our mom said they helped us get good grades in social studies."

"She's fine. I gave her a couple of extra treats. I'm happy to know my books have helped with your schoolwork." *Aunt Tillie, your theory on how to teach kids to enjoy history is still working.* "This is my friend Shane Walker."

Serenity approached the picnic table and held out her book to Shane. "You're the hero who saved Winnie. I know you're not in this book, but it's about a hero named Paul Revere. He risked his life to save the colonists and warned them the British were coming at the start of the Revolutionary War. Could you please sign it for me?"

Unsure of how to handle the young girl's request, Shane shifted his gaze from Serenity to Taylor.

"Thank you for the honor, but I'm not a hero. I consider myself more of a Good Samaritan. Ms. Payne authored the book. I think she should sign it."

What did Shane have against the word *hero*?

"I'll be happy to sign both of your books," Taylor said to the kids. "I hope you'll join me tomorrow night for Reading with Tillie around the campfire. A special cat will be putting in an appearance."

They broke into smiles at that announcement.

"See you tomorrow evening," Taylor said after signing their books. "The sun is starting to set, so go right home."

They started walking back to their cabin, but Serenity stopped and turned around. "Mr. Shane, I still think you're a hero."

Taylor was about to broach the subject of why he had an aversion to being referred to as a hero, but he spoke up first.

"Does this happen often? I mean, children stopping by every time you camp?" He dipped his head toward the side of the bus. "That vehicle is a definite attention-getter."

"Yes, and I really don't mind. Ten months out of the year, I teach history to middle-school children.

~ 34 ~

In the summer months, I travel to national parks and historic sites to gather information for my books."

"I find this all fascinating. How do you decide on which place to go?"

Spending time with Shane had been so enjoyable. She didn't want the evening to end. There was so much more she wanted to know about him. He'd cleverly let her do most of the talking, much different from dates she'd been on where the guys had loved to just talk about themselves. As soon as they'd learned she was an author, they told her all about how they dreamed of writing the great American novel. She'd tolerated their babbling with a smile.

Trying to get Shane to talk about himself was like trying to get water out of a dry well. Even though she knew about his heroic military heritage, she pretended ignorance when she brought up his family. He gave her a vague answer his father and brother lived on the East Coast, and he hadn't seen them in months. That just raised more questions.

As for future plans, he was undecided. Her frustration with her dinner guest was mounting. In all fairness, she had no right to pry into his personal life.

Earlier, he'd expressed interest in how she'd ended up with her *Adventures with Tillie* bus. Showing him her aunt's journal would be a great place to start.

"Are you in a hurry to get back to Liberty?"

"You mean the dog who is looking out the window at us? I think she might be jealous."

Taylor couldn't help but smile at the doggy peeping Tom. "I'll make a deal with you. I'll tell you

~ 35 ~

how I came to be driving this bus around, but you have to tell me about Liberty. Why don't you bring her over so she and Winnie can get better acquainted? She just might be a new character for my series. My invitation comes with coffee and dessert."

"Sounds good, but first let me help you clean up. Word of advice: Don't let that sweet face fool you. She cons me out of hamburgers all the time."

"Too late. I have an extra one."

*****

Two powerful paws landing on Shane's shoulders almost knocked him backward when he opened the door. "You're definitely going on a diet. Sit, stay."

Liberty plopped her butt on the floor, and Shane bent to one knee. "You've been invited next door, but I need you to be on your best behavior. This lady is very special. We're going to be here for a few days, and I'd like to spend more time with her. She also made you a hamburger."

The dog woofed in agreement.

He walked to the back of the trailer to get the leash stored in the metal storage cabinet he'd built into the side of the wall. Taylor was nice, very nice. Beautiful, funny, interesting. To his delight, she'd made him laugh.

Earlier, Taylor had encouraged him to talk about himself, but he'd always considered himself a private person and refrained from offering personal information. Dane and his father were the boastful ones in the family, capitalizing on their family's naval dedication. Talk about himself? He'd wait to see what the next couple of days brought.

Just before Taylor opened the door to Shane's knock, he tugged lightly on Liberty's leash. "Remember, behave."

His pretty hostess had set out two cups, additional paper plates and napkins on the small dining table. One end was attached to the wall, making it easy to collapse when not needed.

"Hi, Liberty!" She'd cut up the hamburger and set it on the floor next to the table leg. "This is for you."

With the leash still attached to her collar, his glutton of a dog devoured the hamburger in one second flat. *Wait for it,* he told himself. Liberty sat down and lifted her paw in a form of thank-you.

The smile that filled Taylor's face couldn't have been broader. She got down on one knee and shook the dog's paw before gathering Liberty's snout between her hands. "You're very welcome. You and Winnie will make great pals."

A meow behind him had him turning around. Winnemucca sat on the top shelf of the rolltop desk. She then proceeded to lick her paws.

"Is this the calm before the storm between these two?" Taylor asked, going to the sink to wash her hands. "Pardon my manners. Please sit down."

"Liberty is a former rescue dog. Having been around other dogs and cats, she learned they're not to be threatened in any way. I've seen her carry a cat and a small dog out of a collapsed building."

Taylor poured two cups of freshly brewed coffee and set them on the table. Plastic wrap covered a plate of apple turnovers. How had she known he enjoyed anything made with apples?

"What do you take in your coffee?"

"Black with one sugar."

"Same here," she said and removed the covering from their dessert. "Help yourself. I made these in a hurry."

One bite of the apples laced with cinnamon and sugar was ambrosia. "These are delicious." He finished one and helped himself to another.

"Tell me about Liberty."

He should've seen this coming, but this was about Liberty, not him. A woof came from under the table. Winnie had decided to check out her new friend and had claimed a spot near their feet.

"She's eight years old. I got her when she was six. Liberty suffered a broken leg while rescuing people after an earthquake in Haiti. She's got a rod in her back hind leg. From the way she can run, you'd never know it. They decided to retire her. Dogs like that are then put up for adoption."

"I never could have given up a dog that I'd grown to love. What happened to her handler?"

"He was a close friend and was badly injured in the same search-and-rescue mission. I couldn't let Liberty be adopted by a stranger. She's become my best friend." He meant it with all his heart.

~ 38 ~

"You mean you rescued her from going to someone she didn't know?"

"Let's say we saved each other." He needed to change the direction of this conversation. "Tell me how you got into writing *Adventures with Tillie*."

*****

She moved to the desk and picked up Aunt Tillie's journal, along with two graphic novels. "My aunt taught school for thirty-five years before she retired. History was her expertise, but getting middle-school children to engage was a challenge. What kid is interested in facts, dates, and biographies of people they've never met? This is my aunt's take on George Washington crossing the Delaware River." She handed him one of the graphic novels.

Shane opened the cover and started reading—and kept reading, laughing out loud at something Winnemucca had done in the story. "This is great! What kid wouldn't enjoy reading about history this way?"

"She was able to write six books before she passed away from COPD. I was her only living relative, so I inherited her small estate, which included the bus and Winnemucca. And I took over writing the books, too." Taylor flipped through the pages of the journal to the list of places her aunt had put together. "I've also been following Aunt Tillie's list of places she wanted to go."

"From the checkmarks, you've completed eight more from her original list. That's quite commendable. Have you always wanted to write children's books?"

"I love writing, and my dream is to write foreign espionage, romantic suspense novels. I've already outlined a number of books, but they have to take a back seat until I fulfill Aunt Tillie's legacy. Maybe someday. I'm here now to research a book about Mount Rushmore."

"What's your plan?"

"Tomorrow, I'll pick up a rental car and drive into Keystone to visit the Lincoln Borglum Museum. It gives the full story of the development of the monument. It's a must-see before you go to the actual monument."

"Sounds like you have a good plan. Tomorrow, I have to find an automotive store and places to purchase food and get a haircut. How about I return the favor and cook dinner tomorrow night?"

He'd admitted earlier that he couldn't cook, so why was he offering to fix her dinner? *Maybe he enjoys your company! Whatever he cooks can't be that bad.* "I'd like that, but I don't know when I'll be back to the campground."

He reached for a paper napkin. "Do you have a pencil or a pen I can use? I'll give you my cell number."

Their newly established friendship had progressed a lot faster than she'd anticipated. Was she doing the right thing by giving him her cell number?

~ 40 ~

YES! She ripped the napkin in half and wrote down her number.

"Now, we don't want to overstay our welcome." The minute he stood up, Liberty came out from under the table. "Thank Taylor for the burger."

The dog sat and once again thrust out a paw.

"Oh, you are a love." She grinned. "I can see it now. You'll be in the book I write about the Liberty Bell."

She waited until they'd reached the door to Shane's trailer before turning off the outside lights. It had been an enjoyable evening, and she was looking forward to spending more time with Shane.

Winnie hopped up onto the counter.

"What do you think of our new friends? Here I go again, talking to a cat. I need to come up with a special story, considering your new friend's name."

She rinsed the cups they'd used for their coffee and put the rest of the apple turnovers in the refrigerator.

It had really been a good night, but Shane Walker was still an enigma.

Chapter 4

"What do you mean you don't have a reservation for a rental car listed under my name?"

Taylor stared at the woman behind the counter in the car rental area of the reception center. Three other people behind her were also waiting to get their cars. "I made the reservation online four months ago! I even got a confirmation number." Taylor handed the woman a printout of the reservation.

"Ms. Parish, this rental is for August. That's next month." She returned the copy to Taylor with an understanding smile.

"Oh no," she moaned in disappointment, staring down at her obvious mistake. "I never double-checked the reservation. My apologies. Would you have a car available anyway?"

"I'm sorry, Ms. Parish, we have nothing available."

She could switch her plans around. "How about tomorrow?"

"Sorry, we're fully booked to the end of the month."

"Come on, lady, move it along."

She quickly turned around to glower at the bad-tempered man behind her. "Like you've never made a mistake!"

"Ms. Parish, I can put your name on a waiting list in case we get any cancellations."

~ 42 ~

"Thank you. I'd appreciate that. Please cancel my rental for next month. I'll be in Philadelphia then."

Thoroughly disappointed, she walked outside, disgusted with herself. A row of green-painted wooden benches lined the porch of the log building. She sat for a few minutes. Now what? The day was wide open, and she hated to waste time. The plans for this evening's reading were all set.

Across the way was a small luncheonette with umbrella-shaded picnic tables on the porch. To the right was the Chuck Wagon Barbecue restaurant. Shane would probably take advantage of those amenities, she decided.

A chalkboard close to where she was sitting listed the day's activities. For a small fee, the campground offered transportation via retired school buses to take campers to the national park to view the popular nighttime activities. She'd already put her name on the list for the Fourth of July program to honor American heroes.

Had Shane signed up? Dinner last night had been so enjoyable. He was handsome, personable, friendly, though standoffish when it came to talking about himself. She still couldn't read him. Why hadn't he shared with her he was in the Navy?

She needed to make sure Shane attended the Fourth of July celebration. *Stop right there, girl,* the commonsense part of her brain argued. *You're assuming too much. You just met the man. Maybe he doesn't like crowds. Maybe he's made other plans.*

~ 43 ~

Maybe he doesn't like fireworks. Maybe he just needs a nudge in the right direction.

She put her hands to her knees and shoved up from the bench. "I'm going to do it."

Burt was standing at the reservation desk, signing a family up for a rafting adventure.

"Hi, Ms. Parish. You're going to have a full house tonight," Burt said. "The kids are so excited."

"Winnemucca and I are looking forward to it. I have a special request. Could you please check to see if Shane Walker signed up for a seat on the bus to attend the Fourth of July celebration at Mount Rushmore? He's the gentleman who saved Winnie."

"You mean the hero." He called up the list on his computer. "His name isn't on the list, but I just got a single cancellation. Should I put his name down?"

"Absolutely." She opened the small purse on her hip, removed her wallet and handed the manager of the resort a five-dollar bill. "My treat. Thanks so much. I'll let him know he's got a reservation."

"Don't forget to take advantage of our pancake breakfast in the activity center next to the pool every morning from eight to ten o'clock. Payment is by donation only to the Ladies Auxiliary for our volunteer fire department."

"Thanks, Burt. Since my plans for the day changed, I think I'll head on over there."

Surrounded by green-covered mountains and pleasant air, she made her way down the paved road to the other end of the campground. The campsites were filled with a variety of trailers. The voices of happy

~ 44 ~

children let everyone know they were enjoying the amenities in the playground. She paused to watch a young boy come down a bright yellow snakelike tube. He landed feet first on a mound of rubber pieces covering the ground. Laughing, he went to do it again, but stopped and waved to Taylor. Recognizing her, he ran over.

"Morning, Luca. You're up early."

"We already had pancakes, and they were great! We're going to pan for gold this afternoon! See you tonight!"

Kids and their enthusiasm. She loved it.

The Western theme continued in the activity center when she opened one of the double doors. Long tables and benches had been set up chuckwagon-style. Ladies dressed in long frontier-style dresses served freshly made pancakes. The scent of frying bacon awakened her tastebuds.

Female interest had her scanning the room for her hunky neighbor. This was a meal he wouldn't have to cook. Disappointed at not seeing him, she reached for a plastic tray at the same time that another hand did.

"Fancy meeting you here, Ms. Parish."

Pitter-patter, be still my heart. Her day was definitely looking up. "Why am I not surprised to see you here, Mr. Walker?"

"I happen to love pancakes." He passed her a white Styrofoam plate and a napkin wrapped around a plastic fork and knife. "I thought you'd be on the road by now."

~ 45 ~

"My plans changed." She wasn't able to tell him why at that moment. A woman wearing a wide-brimmed bonnet asked if he was the hero who'd saved the famous cat yesterday. Taylor rolled her lips inward and quickly looked away. Apparently, his reputation as a hero had spread. It wasn't her imagination his fingers had tightened around the napkin roll of utensils.

His lips strained in a tense smile while the server placed six pancakes on his plate. The bacon was on the house. Taylor wanted only two pancakes with her bacon. Before she could put money in the donation jar, Shane put in a twenty-dollar bill.

"You didn't have to pay for my breakfast," she said when they found an open space at the end of one of the tables.

"I know I didn't, but I wanted to. Sit, and I'll get us coffee."

She waited for him to return to the table before she started eating. The pancakes were light and delicious. Shane consumed all six of his pancakes and five slices of bacon.

"The food was great, but the company was even better." He grinned and winked.

Don't blush. Too late.

"Why did you change your plans?" he asked.

"I rented a car, but put down the wrong date. There aren't any other rentals to be had."

He finished the rest of the coffee in his paper cup. "Too bad you don't know of someone who has a set of wheels and can drive you around."

My hero! She bit back the words. "Shane, you have your own plans. I don't want to impose."

"That's the thing. I don't have a set schedule. My to-do list is finding a piece for my classic motorcycle, do laundry, buy food, and possibly get a haircut. I hadn't planned to do the tourist thing."

Not do the tourist thing? What was the sense in coming to one of the most popular areas in America if not to experience history? "Shane, I'm not being nosy, but why did you decide to come to Mount Rushmore?"

"I didn't *plan* to come to Mount Rushmore specifically. This was the only place I could get a reservation. One of my best friends got married over the weekend in Rapid City, and I was in his wedding party."

Her love of American history determined his reasoning for coming here was… She didn't know what. Her teacher senses were fired up. He was going to get a crash course about the history of Mount Rushmore.

"I'll accept your offer. In exchange, I'll provide lunch and dinner and pay for your gas. I'll give you a copy of the itinerary I put together. I also want to see the Crazy Horse Memorial that's still in development. If it's too much, let me know."

*****

Bumping into Taylor Parish in the breakfast line had been a surprise and very much welcomed. She looked cute in blue denim shorts and a yellow sleeveless blouse. Small yellow bows adorned the ends of her long braids. The laces in her sneakers were decorated with yellow smiley faces. She appeared more like one of her students than the teacher.

He'd had no plans to check out the free breakfast, but he'd run out of coffee. When he'd walked Liberty in the dog area, he'd noticed campers going into the recreation hall. Then he'd recalled reading about the pancake breakfast in the brochure he'd been given when he checked in.

And there she was with her beautiful smile. If she'd asked him to take her to the moon, he would've have said, *Let me see what I can do*. Her enthusiasm was infectious. His time here would not be boring. He liked her—a lot.

"I'll think of you as my personal tour guide. Another thing I planned to do was drive the Needles Highway on my motorcycle. She's a classic Harley I purchased four months ago, and I've been restoring her."

"So you're a mechanic?"

"I've a degree in mechanical engineering, so I enjoy working with machines and engines, old and new ones."

"Where did you graduate from?"

Torpedo. Direct hit. He already anticipated her surprised reaction. "Annapolis."

Brown eyes widened in recognition. "Annapolis, as in the US Naval Academy? Are you in the Navy?"

~ 48 ~

His explanation was going to be short and to the point. "I put in twenty years and retired six months ago. Now the only vessels I steer are my truck and motorcycle."

Her arm stretched across the table, and she threaded her fingers through his. "Shane, that's very commendable. Thank you for your service. When you have time, I'd love to hear about your career."

"There's nothing commendable about it. I enjoyed being in the Navy and achieved the rank of lieutenant. Now it's time for me to do what I'd like to do."

"Giving twenty years of your life in the service of our country is admirable," she argued.

That's your opinion. He stood up and collected their garbage. "What's your first stop, and when do you want to leave?"

"Shane, why do I get the feeling I've offended you in some way?"

Taylor's innocent question stirred up the bitterness he'd kept locked away. She didn't deserve to be treated badly. It hadn't taken long for him to screw up a friendship with a woman he really liked and wanted to know a lot better. He ran the tip of his finger down her soft cheek.

"Sorry. I'm being a selfish jerk. Living alone with a dog for six months, I've become my own worst enemy. Again, my apologies."

"Since it's just me and my cat, I understand. If you ever feel like talking, I'm happy to bend an ear."

"If that ever happened, you'd be crippled over."

~ 49 ~

They walked outside together and headed for their campsites. He liked that she wrapped her hand around his arm.

"I know we haven't started our adventure, but thanks for going with me."

"My pleasure. I have to take Liberty for a walk, and then I'm all yours. What's our first stop?"

"Like I mentioned last evening, we're going to Keystone to visit the Borglum Museum. I want to know about how Mount Rushmore came to be. Everyone knows about the carved faces, but they need to know about the artist and his son who created the memorial. After that, I'd like to walk the Presidential Trail. It's like a boardwalk and provides a close-up view of the memorial. You'll see it on my itinerary, but tomorrow night I want to attend the thirty-minute program at dusk that describes the construction of the memorial."

He pulled back slightly, urging her to stop. "When you said you had this thing planned out, you weren't kidding. Have you worked into your schedule time to eat and sleep?"

Taylor jammed her hands on her hips. "Shane Walker, don't you dare tell me you've changed your mind!"

Her beautiful brown eyes were wide with challenge. All this time, he'd been stringing her along. He tapped her on the tip of her nose. "Ms. Taylor, you must be a heck of a teacher. Since we're going on this grand adventure together, let me ask you this. Who is Doane Robinson?"

~ 50 ~

She grasped the end of one of her braids and shook her head, realizing she'd been had. "You snake! You've been pulling my leg all this time! Enlighten me, Lieutenant Walker."

He was momentarily stunned by her calling him by his naval rank, but put it aside. "Doane Robinson is known as the Father of Mount Rushmore. It was his idea for the carvings in the Black Hills. He wanted to create an attraction to draw people to his state. He originally favored Western heroes. John Fremont, Lewis and Clark, Sacagawea, and Buffalo Bill Cody. Shall I go on?"

"Okay, smart guy, who decided George Washington, Thomas Jefferson, Abraham Lincoln, and Theodore Roosevelt should be on the memorial?"

"Gutzon Borglum, the artist. Okay, teacher, why is it called Mount Rushmore?"

She tapped him on his chest with the tip of her finger and grinned. "It was named for New York lawyer Charles Rushmore, who traveled to the Black Hills in 1885 to inspect mining claims in the region."

They started walking again. "You've done your research."

"Apparently, so have you," she returned.

From the accusing stare she sent his way, he prepared himself for another round of personal questions. Peeping Tom Liberty's happy barks greeted them when they got to his trailer. "If you don't come in and say hello, she'll be hurt. I'll give you a tour."

"I'd like that."

~ 51 ~

"Let me go in first. Liberty's greetings are very enthusiastic. She still hasn't learned not to jump up on people."

Shane opened the door and braced himself for the German shepherd's *I missed you* energy. "Stop! We have a guest, and don't jump!" he ordered, trying to dodge doggy kisses to his cheek.

"Sweet Liberty!" Taylor called.

That was all the fickle dog needed to hear to transfer her warm greeting to Taylor. The force of her jumping up on Taylor was so strong, the dog shoved her backward. Shane reacted quickly and reached out with both arms to try to catch her. They landed on the floor with her flat on top of him.

It had been a long time since he'd felt a warm, soft, feminine body. Taylor Parish was exceptional in every way. He wasn't familiar with the fragrances women preferred, but whatever she was wearing was pleasant and not breath-clawingly strong. The bushy end of one of her braids tickled his nose. His arms continued to gather her close. "Are you hurt?"

Chapter 5

It had been a long time since she'd enjoyed the closeness of touching a hard, muscled, male body. The brief relationship she'd had with a fellow teacher had ended four years ago, and she'd decided to concentrate on her career.

Shane Walker was built and solid in all the right places. He wasn't even breathing hard when they landed on the floor. A hint of a dark shadow on his cheeks suggested he hadn't shaved this morning, giving him the rugged look she preferred. What was wrong with her? She should be shoving off him, but…

The thin scar that extended from the corner of his eye to his temple drew her attention. With a boldness that surprised even her, she brought the tip of her finger to the scar and traced it up to his hairline.

"Where did you get this hero wound?"

"It's not a hero wound."

Short, blunt and to the point. She needed to stop using that word. The strong hold he had on her body eased. She rolled off him and stood up. "Since you have an aversion to the word 'hero,' I'll rephrase my question. How did you get that scar?"

"In a bar fight with a bunch of bikers in Baha, California." As soon as Shane stood up, Liberty bumped her head against his knee. He gave her gentle pats on the head.

~ 53 ~

"Really?" The twinkle in his eye was a sure sign he was once again teasing her. She challenged him, raising a brow. "How about the truth?"

"When I was seventeen, I attended the Naval Academy Prep School. It prepares you for going into the Naval Academy and helps to strengthen your academic and physical skills."

"You went from prep school into the Naval Academy?"

"It was expected of me. My family has served in the Navy since the Revolutionary War. The Department of the Navy was formed in 1775 by General Washington to defend the colonies from British attack. As a teacher of American history, you probably know all this."

She dipped her head in a nod. "I knew about the origins of the Navy, but now I learned you're part of a long line of military personage. Tell me about your scar."

"We were on a weeklong survival exercise on land and sea. My buddy Benny Acosta, the one who got married over the weekend, hadn't secured a line properly when we were belaying down a mountain. He was literally dangling from the end of the rope. I went down to help him and encountered a jagged edge of a rock. I bled, wore a couple of butterfly bandages for a few days. No biggie."

A sixth sense said his explanation was full of holes. She refrained from saying, *Shane, you were a hero.*

~ 54 ~

"My beverage selection is slim. I only have bottled water."

"Thanks. I'll take a rain check. Your place is very nice. The kitchenette and dining area are more spacious than I imagined."

"I purchased the trailer from a US park ranger. He was upgrading to a Class C. He needed a different arrangement to accommodate his family."

Taylor got the impression he was accustomed to order. Was it part of his military conditioning? The kitchen counter area was clutter-free. Not even a cup or glass in the sink. Peeking into his bedroom, she saw the queen-size bed was neatly made. On the wall was a flat-screen television.

"I'm being nosy. What's back there?"

"The main reason I purchased a toy hauler."

Shane opened a door to a huge open space, answering the question she'd had about the design of toy haulers. His fingers wrapped around the handle of a Harley that took up half of the space.

"This Black Beauty is a 1991 Harley-Davidson Ultra Classic. The extra-large sidecar can hold an adult and has adjustable suspension to compensate for a load. I got the sidecar so I can take Liberty with me."

"This brings back a happy memory from when I was a little girl. A motorcycle cop would come to our elementary school every year for police safety week. Officer Baudelaire would give the kids a ride in his sidecar."

"Would you like to go for a ride sometime?"

~ 55 ~

Her eyes opened wide at his invitation. "Really? I'd love that."

His cell phone rang, and he pulled it from his pocket. A scowl immediately appeared on his face. "Excuse me."

She wondered what that was all about. This was his happy place and where he spent most of his time, she determined. Along with storage for his motorcycle, the interior of the trailer was a mini workshop, complete with a metal workbench secured against an exterior wall. Bins were neatly marked with their contents. A handheld acetylene torch and heavy gloves and protective goggles sat in the center of the workbench.

She didn't recognize any of the other tools securely stationed to the pegboard above the workbench. A number of framed photos drew her closer. Three men stood with their arms around one another to indicate close camaraderie. She recognized one man as Shane. All were dressed in black wetsuits and held flippers. Face masks dangled around their necks. Air tanks were still attached to their backs.

She'd just gotten another of her questions answered. He'd been a Navy diver.

"Sorry, that was my father," Shane said as he shoved the phone into the back pocket of his jeans. "Apparently, he's coming my way for the holiday weekend. He's been asked to give a speech at the Fourth of July program at the monument. My brother is coming with him."

He showed none of the happiness one might expect a man to feel when he found out he was going to be able to spend some time with his family. This raised more questions about Shane Walker.

"Do they plan to stay with you?"

"No. Plus, I don't have room. He'll call me when they get to their hotel. He wants me to join them for dinner."

She touched the back of his hand with her fingertips. "Shane, I know this isn't any of my business, but why don't you want to see your family?"

He paced in the short space for a few moments, apparently struggling with whether to answer her question. "We've been at odds for quite a while. He hates that I retired and wants to reinstate me. My brother, Dane, and I are twins, but I was born first. Dane is the fair-haired, can-do-no-wrong child and has no problem sucking up to fame and glory. I enjoyed my time in the Navy and loved serving my country."

He jabbed the tip of his thumb into the center of his chest. "Now it's time for me to do what I want to do!"

"And what is it you want to do?"

"I'm still trying to figure that out."

She'd learned a little bit more about him. He'd been expected to follow in the footsteps of his elders, and he didn't believe in heroes.

"Taylor, again my apologies for spouting off. I shouldn't trouble you with my family problems."

"It's okay. I told you if you needed to bend my ear, I'm available." She threw back her shoulders, keeping them stiff and straight. "See? Still standing tall. In all honesty, you've served your country with honor and have every right to move on to something else. I admire you, and I'll only say this once more—thank you for your service."

"Thanks. If I see one of your shoulders start to dip, I'll back off," he said and winked.

"Now, we really must get going. Can you be ready to leave in a half hour?"

"Not a problem. I'll take Liberty for a walk and come to your bus."

*****

Shane removed the sunglasses he'd shoved above the peak of his soft baseball cap and put them on when they walked outside. Tourists were already in line at the front of the building for the next showing. The bright sun was blinding, and the difference between the air-conditioned air inside and the temperature outside was striking.

The time they'd spent inside the Lincoln Borglum Museum, followed by the movie, had been longer than he'd anticipated. The idea to carve faces into a mountain had been mind-blowing, but the determination of man couldn't be stopped.

Taylor took off the light sweater she'd worn inside the building and tied it around her waist. "I did my research about the creation of the monument, but between all the displays and the historic movie that was so real, I felt like I was right there." She retrieved her sunglasses from her hip pouch.

"I, too, found out so much. From 1927 to October 1941, Gutzon and four hundred workers sculpted the colossal monument. The actual workers were miners, not artists," he pointed out.

"When you think about it, miners were perfect for the job, as they knew how to use dynamite. About 450,000 tons of stone were removed, and 90% of the carving was done with dynamite. The cost was a million dollars, and not one person died while working on it."

"That was the price way back then, but when you compare it to today's cost of living, it would be more like $14 million. Before you ask how I know, I read it on one of the display cards," he said.

"I asked about erosion of the monument, but erosion is one inch every ten thousand years. There is yearly maintenance to seal the cracks and reseal patches that have pulled away from the caulking. The stone is also cleaned."

"What's next on your agenda?" he asked.

"The Presidential Trail. It's only half a mile. It offers an up close and personal view of the monument."

The walk would normally take twenty minutes, but took longer because of the number of tourists. Protective post-and-rail fencing on either side made the path easy to follow. Because of the crowd, they had to wait their turn to read the displays in the glass-topped cases along the trail. Fortunately, the number of visitors thinned out when it came to walking the numerous sets of steps that took people closer to the monument.

Taylor stopped and leaned against a railing before removing a bottle of water from her hip pouch. She passed a second one to him. "No one warned us there would be this many sets of steps." She took a long drink, along with a deep breath. "What are you? Superman? You aren't even breathing heavy."

"Thanks. I never thought to bring a bottle of water." He removed the cap and took a long drink. "I run every morning and swim whenever I get a chance. It's hard to do laps when so many people are in the pool, especially kids. If you're too tired, we can stop."

"No, I'm good."

He watched her take another long drink, deciding she could use a few more minutes to rest. He braced his back and folded his arms across his chest. A couple of kids ran past them, going up the steps two at a time. He might be in good physical shape, but they had a lot more energy.

"Okay, Ms. Taylor, we came away with a lot of knowledge, but what's the one thing that impressed the teacher in you, other than the monument itself?"

She tented her fingers, shifted her eyes to look up at the four faces that made up the monument, then turned to face him. "That space between Presidents Lincoln and Roosevelt has become more obvious to me after learning about the fifth sculpture that never made it there. In 1937, Congress proposed a fifth face be sculpted—Susan B. Anthony. She obviously didn't make it." Taylor paused and actually stamped her foot.

"She was the leader of the women's suffrage movement in the 1800s and helped women finally get the right to vote. Then a bunch of male chauvinists rescinded the bill, stating the construction was over a decade in progress, and they didn't want to, let's say, upset the applecart. What an honor it would have been to all women to state all men and women should be treated equally."

He didn't laugh at her diatribe since he agreed with her. It was just the way she went about expressing her opinion. "I'm sure Susan would be proud you spoke up on her behalf, but I can think of something you could do to support her. Why doesn't Tillie write about Susan B. Anthony and why her face never made it onto the monument?"

Shane was overwhelmed when she wrapped her arms around his neck and hugged him tight. She jumped back before he could return the hug.

"That's a fabulous idea!" Excitement bubbled out of her. "That book will follow the one I plan to write about Betsy Ross. Liberty will be making her debut in that novel. I'll follow up with where Betsy and Liberty meet Susan."

He didn't recall seeing anything about Susan B. Anthony on her aunt's bucket list, but decided not to bring it up. "If you're ready, let's go to the top and take a few pictures. Then maybe we can get some lunch and find a place for me to grocery shop."

~ 61 ~

A little after four o'clock, they got back to the campground. Lunch had been slices of pizza at a local place. When they'd first driven into Keystone, the town had reminded him of a typical Western town, with long wooden porches lining the stores on either side of the street. The chamber of commerce had kept the Western flavor with old-fashioned signs on the wood-framed buildings.

Taylor had also done some food shopping at a small, local food store. From the amount of food they'd purchased, neither of them would starve. The automotive store hadn't had the part he needed for his motorcycle, but they put in a special order. He could come back tomorrow afternoon.

He was actually surprised to find an old-fashioned men's barbershop, complete with a red-and-white-striped pole out front. The barber took off a good amount of hair, and Shane no longer felt like a caveman.

Since his hands were full of bags, Liberty didn't give him her customary bulldozer jump. "How's my girl?" He pulled out a bone and handed it to her. "Amuse yourself with this, and then I'll take you for a walk."

He'd barely finished putting the perishables away when his phone signaled an incoming text. *Arriving at hotel tomorrow afternoon. Plan to meet with me and your brother for dinner. Select a place, and we'll meet you there.*

Knowing his father's and brother's dining preferences, they would expect five-star gourmet.

~ 62 ~

When he and Taylor had been in Keystone, he'd seen a sign for Red Garter Saloon. He Googled the name, and photos of the restaurant came up. The waitresses dressed like dance hall girls and the waiters gamblers. Just what he had in mind.

A bump on his knee reminded him he had to take the dog for a walk. "Liberty, sweetheart, I'm going to take much pleasure in irritating my father and brother!"

Chapter 6

If teachers had looked like Taylor Parish when he'd gone to school, no kid would have wanted to play hooky. Of course, that was just his opinion, though five rows of bleachers were filled with families who hung on every word Taylor was saying, and she'd only just begun her talk.

The sun had gone down a half hour ago. Torches surrounded the area, their flames dancing in the gentle evening breeze. Taylor had asked him to be the official keeper of the "stars" of *Adventures with Tillie*. Since she'd decided to introduce Liberty in her next two books, she'd asked if he would mind if she introduced the German shepherd to her fans. Once her talk was over, the children would be able to meet both the stars, Liberty, and Winnemucca. Said cat was in an oversize carrier near Shane's feet and Liberty sat beside him.

Parents would also be able to purchase the books in the series at a very reduced rate of only two dollars. That the children enjoy reading was more important to her than the money.

She'd also blown him away when he'd met her at the bus to help carry the books over to the area with the bleachers. Her long-fringed dress with colorful beads was authentic Native American clothing, as well as her soft-soled moccasins, which were also decorated with colorful beads. Strips of leather entwined the length of her long braids. A turquoise necklace completed her authentic outfit.

Taylor was amazing, and spending time with her had been so enjoyable. She'd brought him happiness he'd never expected to find. He didn't want to think about how much he would miss her when they parted ways in a few days.

"Tonight, before I read a story," Taylor said to her audience, "I'd like you to know how Winnemucca got her name. Can anyone guess?"

A young boy in front raised his hand. "There's a city in Nevada with that name. My grandparents live there."

"You're correct. The city was named after Chief Winnemucca from the Northern Paiute tribe. His name means 'one moccasin.' He had a daughter, Sarah Winnemucca. That's who Winnie is named after. She was the first Native American woman known to secure a copyright to publish a book in the English language. Her book, *Life Among the Piute's*, is an autobiographical account of her people's experiences during their first forty years of contact with white explorers and settlers."

Taylor nodded at Shane, their prearranged signal that he was to bring the critters center stage. "Behave, and no barking," he warned. He picked up the cat carrier and set it next to Taylor. He turned to go back to his seat.

"No, please stay. Hold on to Winnie when I take her out of the crate." Taylor bent to one knee and patted the dog on the head. "Now, I've a very special treat. I want to introduce you to the newest character in my books. Meet Liberty."

The kids and their parents clapped in greeting. Shane's ham of a dog barked in response.

"She's a hero, a former rescue dog who had to be retired because of an injury. She'll be going on a few adventures with Winnemucca. The next book in the series is about…" Taylor paused and held up the roughly drawn cover of a graphic novel. "Winnie and Liberty help Betsy Ross make the first American flag."

Winnie wiggled in his arms, but he gave the cat soothing pats on the head. "Don't worry, Winnie, you're still the main star."

"It would be remiss of me not to introduce you to Liberty's owner, who has given me permission to add Liberty as a character."

Droplets of sweat formed on his brow, and they weren't brought on by the bonfire behind them. She'd never said she would draw attention to him.

"It is my honor to introduce Lieutenant Shane Walker of the US Navy, retired."

His lips formed a tense smile. A number of spectators called out, "Thank you for your service."

Luca, sitting in the front row, stood up and loudly announced, "He's the hero who saved Winnemucca from the tree."

The crowd started clapping, and Liberty added her doggy two cents.

She silently mouthed the word, "Sorry," before she lifted the cat from his arms. "Thanks. I'll take it from here. Winnie will stay on my lap when I read to the children. Will I see you at breakfast?"

"I'll take Liberty for a walk and then head back to my trailer. See you around."

The activity around the campfire had drawn a lot of people away from their trailers. Only two dogs were running around the doggy area. As soon as he opened the gate and removed her leash, Liberty ran right over to the beagle and Jack Russell terrier. The owner occupied the bench.

Shane was in a foul mood and had no intention of being the friendly camper, but the older gentleman patted the empty space beside him. "Have a seat, young man." He held out his hand. "James Berweiler, sergeant, retired, US Air Force. Thank you for your service."

Being in a lousy mood, Shane hadn't noticed the insignia on the man's hat. He was a Vietnam veteran. Now here was a true hero.

"Thank you for your service, also. How did you know I was in the Navy?"

"When I was walking toward the dog-run area, I heard that young lady introduce you. I heard you're a hero. You rescued a cat from a tree. That was very kind of you. I hope you plan to attend the Fourth of July ceremony."

"I wasn't planning to, and I'm not a hero. The cat ran after a squirrel, and my dog ran after the both of them."

"Whether or not you're a hero, you must attend the ceremony. It includes a talk about the presidents, stressing what each of them did in history to earn their place. This year, they've expanded the show, and the US Air Force Band will be playing patriotic songs. Then all veterans in the audience are invited onto the stage to give their name and branch of service. The band pays taps while the American flag is lowered, and there's a fireworks display. It's going to be a wonderful tribute to veterans. I've been coming here for the past twenty years just for this program."

Shane leaned forward, resting his arms on his knees, and watched Liberty run up and down a doggy ramp. The other two dogs followed. "It sounds wonderful, but I'll pass."

The weight of the aged airman's hand settled on Shane's shoulder. "Son, aren't you proud that you served your country?"

"Sergeant Berweiler, my entire family has served in the US Navy since the Revolutionary War. I don't need to be honored for my service."

"That's a shame, Lieutenant Walker. From one service man to another, I think you're being selfish."

Selfish? I did what I was supposed to do.

"When you walk onto that stage, it's not just about you. You're honoring your family and all those Navy seamen who gave up their lives at Pearl Harbor, the Battle of the Chesapeake, the Battle of Fort Henry, just to name a few. I'm not a hero, but when I step out onto that stage, I'm honoring those who fought beside me and those who never made it home."

This time, his bad mood couldn't be blamed on someone calling him a hero. What the retired Vietnam vet had said was something he'd never considered. Hero vs. honor. He'd lost a number of friends in Desert Storm and Desert Shield. A war was now going on in his head.

Mr. Berweiler stood up and whistled. Both the beagle and the Jack Russell terrier came over and held still while he attached their leashes. "It was nice talking to you, Lieutenant Walker. Think about what I said. I'd be proud to stand beside you on that stage. Have a good night."

"Come on, Liberty, my friend, let's go home. Before I can think about going on a stage, I have to deal with my father and brother."

*****

The book Taylor read to the kids was about George Washington crossing the Delaware River in December 1776 during the Revolutionary War, the first book Aunt Tillie had written. It fit the moment, considering George Washington's face was on Mount Rushmore. The story was well received.

As soon as she'd gotten back from sightseeing, she'd used the drawing program on her computer to sketch out a quick book cover showing Liberty and Winnie with Betsy Ross. She'd also made a few notes about the book she planned to write about Mount Rushmore.

The children were reluctant to say good night to Winnemucca. She was introduced to Luca and Serenity's parents. They offered to help her carry her books back to her bus, but she'd sold out. Signing each book took additional time, but she was happy to do it for the kids. They were doubly happy to get a bookmark with a picture of the bus and Winnemucca.

Once she got back to her bus, she noticed all the lights were out in Shane's trailer. Did he think she'd set him up when she'd introduced him as a retired Navy lieutenant, putting him in an uncomfortable position? She purposely hadn't used the dreaded word *hero*, but she'd had no control over anyone else calling him a hero. What was there to be embarrassed about when surrounded by young families and animals? If only she could get him to open up more.

The time they'd spent together today was wonderful. They'd bantered like comfortable old friends teasing each other. His suggestion she write a book featuring Susan B. Anthony as a character was something she'd never given any thought to.

He'd laughed when she'd told him to tell the barber not to take off too much hair. She liked it longer. He'd gone a little shorter, but remained his handsome self.

Hopefully, she'd see him at breakfast.

*****

Winnie bumped her head against Taylor's elbow, and she glanced at the time at the bottom of her computer. Eight thirty a.m. She'd been working for almost three hours.

~ 70 ~

"I know you want me to feed you."

Last night, she'd tossed and turned, a dissatisfied sandman customer. Shane Walker had consumed her thoughts as she'd tried to think up some way to cheer him up. Her mind had come up blank. At five thirty, she'd given up on trying to sleep, made a cup of coffee and sat at her computer to work on the outlines for the next two books. The interaction between Winnie and Liberty was going so smoothly woofing and meowing filled her ears.

A knock on her door had her fingers pausing on the keys. She looked up, and happiness rejuvenated her tired body. The handsome face of Shane Walker was visible through the glass at the top of the door. One hand clutched a bunch of wildflowers. The other held a foil-covered plate. Still in her shorty pj's, she grabbed her robe off the back of the bathroom door, finger-combed her hair and hurried to open the door.

"Good morning," she greeted before Liberty brushed the side of her leg. She bent down and gave the dog a kiss on the top of her head. "This is a pleasant surprise. Come in."

Shane held out the bouquet first. "This is my apology for being a grump, and here are some warm breakfast rolls to enjoy with a cup of coffee."

"You picked wildflowers for me? Shane, that was so thoughtful of you."

"There aren't any places around here to purchase flowers, so I had to improvise."

She brushed her cheek against the petals of a white daisy. "Mother Nature was your florist." A delicious scent of cinnamon teased her nose. "You baked?"

"They're cinnamon rolls from a can. I hope I didn't wake you."

She set the warm plate on the table in the kitchen area. "No. I beat the sunrise this morning. Couldn't sleep. I've been thinking about my neighbor, wondering if I'd see him again." She found a tall vase under the kitchen sink and filled it with water. The colorful flowers perked her up even more.

"Sorry, Taylor. I've a lot on my mind and am not in the best mood."

"Sit, and I'll make us coffee." She set two paper plates and their coffee mugs on the table before sitting across from him. The white icing he'd spread over the rolls was still oozing with sugary goodness.

One bite of deliciousness caused her to moan. "So good!"

"Would you believe my grandfather used to make them from scratch? But I took the easy way out. Along with apologizing for my rudeness last evening, I've also come to ask a favor."

"No apology necessary. I understand you need to deal with things that irritate you in your own way. What's your favor?"

"I'm meeting my father and brother this evening for dinner, and I'd like you to join us."

Knowing a little about the tension between him and his father, Taylor understood he was putting her in the position of buffer between them. That was okay. It would give her a better picture of the Walker family.

"I'd like that. Where do you plan to meet them?" The twinkle in his eye was a sure sign he was up to something.

"The Red Garter Saloon in Keystone. The waiters and waitresses dress in authentic Western saloon costumes. I made a reservation for seven o'clock."

"I love the idea, but I take it by the look in your eye your father doesn't have a sense of humor."

"No. He's all about five-star gourmet all the way."

Taylor thought of something that would definitely cheer Shane up, but she'd have to introduce the idea subtly. "I'll do it for a favor. I got up early and got a lot of work done. Can we go for a ride on your Harley?"

The smile she received said he was in favor of her idea. "I, too, was up before the sun, working on my cycle. I hurt my lovely neighbor's feelings and was trying to come up with a way to apologize. I plan to ride the Needles Highway and Iron Mountain Road. It's seventeen miles long, with three hundred fourteen curves, fourteen switchbacks and three pigtails. There are also numerous tunnels. We'll be able to get awesome views of the monument."

"I have no idea what a switchback or a pigtail is other than something in my hair, but I'm sure you'll explain when we get to them. The trip sounds fascinating. I'll pack our lunch in my little cooler."

"I know you're the writer, but this would make a grand adventure for your current book. I can see

Winnie hanging out of a sidecar, taking lots of pictures."

"Are you sure you're not a would-be writer? I love your idea. Tillie will be driving the motorcycle."

Shane shook his head. "Writing is your expertise. Can you be ready to leave around ten o'clock? We'll take our time and make a few stops along the way."

"Perfect." Inside, she bubbled with excitement about getting to spend the rest of the day and evening in the company of a man who had become special to her. Very special. She didn't want to think about how she would feel when they went their separate ways in a few days. He hadn't mentioned where he planned to go next. No harm in suggesting he visit Philadelphia…

*****

He had it all. Freedom, fresh air, scenery meant to be preserved on canvas. Sharing this paradise with his beautiful riding companion made it even more enjoyable. Traveling the S curves and U-shaped switchbacks was more of a challenge with the sidecar, upping the challenge. He understood the concept of a pigtail bridge, where the road looped over itself like an interstate interchange to rapidly gain or drop altitude, but it was the first time he'd experienced driving one.

Because of the face shield on her helmet, he wasn't able to tell if she was enjoying herself. He'd connected them via Bluetooth through his bike, so they were able to talk. The first time they traversed a switchback, she'd squealed in his ear, followed by, "I love this!" A woman after his own heart.

Guiding the cycle through the tunnels drilled into the mountain wasn't difficult, but they were so narrow motor homes and trailers would never be able to fit through them.

They'd just come down from the mountainous area onto a smooth straightaway through Custer State Park, and he wondered why all the cars up ahead had stopped. A number had pulled over to the side of the road.

Taylor let him know what was going on by squealing in his ear, "Look at all those bison! There has to be a couple hundred on either side of the road! There are babies, too! What if one of the bison decides to charge us?"

The thought had also crossed his mind, but he kept it to himself. "We'll go slow and hopefully not provoke them."

"They look pretty docile."

"I'm about to give the teacher a lesson. These bison, also known as buffalo, are wild, no matter how docile they look. You could be gored or trampled. Those guys can weigh up to a ton and stand about six feet tall at the shoulder."

"You know this how?"

"I researched the area for our drive today."

"Of course you did."

The five cars in front of them started to move slowly. He followed suit, but the huge critter who had been grazing on the green grass that bordered the road decided to cross directly in front of them. Taylor's gasp filled his ear. "How fast can a buffalo run?"

"About thirty-five to forty miles an hour." Shane kept a watchful eye on the beast that decided to stand on the double yellow line in the middle of the road. A second one meandered over to join the one in front of them. Now Shane was getting nervous. He kept the engine at idle, but his gloved fingers gripped the handlebars a little tighter.

The temperature was rising as they sat in the open. Sweat formed on his forehead. Hopefully, none of the impatient drivers behind them would beep their horns.

"Do you think if I threw a ham and cheese sandwich on the side of the road, they would move out of the way?"

Shane chuckled lightly. "Sure, but then we'd have a stampede of buffalo going after a sandwich. Winnemucca can do something like that in your book."

"You're filling my head with great ideas!"

Ten minutes later, the buffalo moved to the other side of the road. Still apprehensive, Shane moved by at a crawl, keeping an eye on the beasts just in case any of the other brutes wanted to cross the road. A half mile later, he breathed easier. A sign up ahead indicated a rest stop with restrooms. He decided they could use a break.

Families were enjoying eating at the picnic benches. They found one under the branches of a birch tree. Leave it to Taylor to come prepared, complete with a red-and-white-checked tablecloth. She removed two plastic containers that held their sandwiches from the cooler and pickles. Two bags of chips and bottles of iced tea completed their picnic lunch.

"I'm not going to ask if you're enjoying yourself. You haven't stopped smiling." He finished his sandwich made with a hoagie roll and started on the potato chips. She couldn't see it, but on the inside, his smile was just as huge.

"I'll be perfectly honest and admit I was a little nervous at first, but you're a great driver. No amusement park ride compares to the twisty turns we took. Some sections didn't even have guardrails! Thank you so much for including me in your adventure."

"I'm happy to share it with you."

Taylor opened her bag of chips. "I don't want to rain on our parade, but is there a subject you want to avoid this evening at dinner with your dad and brother?"

He'd been enjoying himself so much, he'd totally forgotten about tonight. "I already know my father will dominate the conversation, thrilled he has a new audience. Don't get me wrong, he's had a great run in the Navy, continuing our family's military tradition. I think he could consider retiring."

"I'll play the devil's advocate here. The Navy has been his whole life, but what would he do if he retired?'

Her question gave him pause, and his mind came up blank. "That's a very good question, and I can honestly say I don't know."

"So tell me about your twin brother." She started nibbling on a chip.

"Dane is Dane. Loves being in the Navy. Walks proud in his uniform that garners the attention of females. Looks for the easy way to either do something or get out of it by making up an excuse. He won't take responsibility if he makes a mistake. It's always the other guy's fault. Loves being the center of attention. If there's praise to be had, he's always first in line."

"Your father doesn't see this?"

"No. Dane does everything my father tells him to do. Dane is the yes son. When I told my father I purchased a motorcycle, he told me to get rid of it. No son of his would ever be a, and I quote, 'Hells Angels biker.' Dane has been engaged twice, but the fiancées disagreed with my father once too often, so they were history."

"I haven't met your family, but I feel sorry for you." Taylor gathered up the containers and tablecloth and returned them to the cooler. "Shane, do you trust me?"

He dipped his head to the side. "Yes. Why?"

"I'm not going to tell you now. On our way back, we need to stop at the Western-clothing shop in Deadwood."

"What are you going to do?"

Chapter 7

Hours later, Taylor released her seat belt as soon as Shane removed his key from the ignition of his truck. "Are you sure I won't shock your father and brother too much?"

He gave her the biggest grin. "Taylor, you're the sexiest-looking biker chic I've ever met."

Heat swept her cheeks. *Sexy biker chick! This is crazy.* She normally didn't do anything to bring attention to herself. *That's why I make all the characters in my books do crazy things. Pulling off a flamboyant stunt like this is something Aunt Tillie would do without hesitation.*

Giving it more thought, she realized it wasn't just her fun-filled day that had brought on this change. That achievement belonged to Shane Walker. Riding seventeen miles of twists, turns, and tunnels and challenging wildlife ten times her size had pulled Taylor out of her boring box.

The Western-clothing shop they'd visited earlier had had everything she needed. He'd laughed out loud when she'd told him what she planned to wear. The stretch jeans were as close as she could get to black leather. The tightness of the black and red bustier that girdled her ribs was a bit uncomfortable. Nickle-size disks decorated her black denim jacket. Not knowing what to do with her hair, she'd left it free-flowing and rolled up a red Western bandanna to create a headband.

Shane's mouth had dropped when he'd picked her up, followed by a big grin. He continued to stare and twirled his finger to get her to turn around so he could see her outfit from all sides.

He'd surprised her with the thin leather strap that she now wore around her neck. He'd added the silver disks. No one had ever referred to her as being sexy.

"From that comment, I take it you've met quite a few biker chicks."

"You're the first, only and last. My father will disapprove of what I'm wearing, too."

Shane had selected Western-cut jeans to wear with his black biker boots. The black string tie and tanned rawhide vest looked great with his white long-sleeve shirt. Marshal Dillon could arrest her anytime.

She needed to make sure he was still in agreement with her crazy idea. She pressed the tips of her fingers to his arm before he got out of the truck. "It's not too late to call this off."

He leaned over the center console and brushed her mouth with a quick kiss. "I'm enjoying not playing by the rules or being concerned about what my father will order me to do. That's why I'm no longer in the military. Let's go shake things up." He put his black Stetson on and opened the door.

The tips of her fingers were now pressed to her tingling mouth. The brief kiss Shane had given her had been nice, but over much too quickly. Things between them were moving very quickly. Common sense said to put on the brakes, but... She was having too much fun and wouldn't mind enjoying more of his kisses.

The butterflies in her stomach went a little crazy when he opened the door for her. "If I embarrass you," she said, "I'll apologize now."

"And I'll apologize for my blowhard of a father. As for my brother, I'll reserve judgment for now."

What have I gotten myself into? she asked herself.

He put a hand to her elbow when they walked up the four steps to the wooden porch that ran the length of the commercial shops. Rinky-tink music could be heard coming from the restaurant. The moment they passed through the authentic swinging doors, the ambience of a true Western saloon continued.

The decor depicted an upscale gambling parlor from the early 1900s. Red-flocked paper covered the walls, blending with the dark wood trim and carved railing of the balcony that encircled the room. Pictures in silver, gold and wood frames flanked wanted posters of gunslingers and gamblers from years past. Just as she'd suspected, the music was coming from a player piano.

The hostess, dressed in an authentic dance hall costume, complete with layers of ruffles on her dress, greeted them at the hostess podium. Protruding from the bun atop her head was a fluffy black and white feather.

~ 81 ~

"Welcome to the Red Garter Saloon."

Shane showed his manners and removed his hat. "We have a reservation for Walker."

"We just seated the other members of your party. Follow me."

Taylor wasn't prepared for him to slip his hand into hers. Mr. Cool, Calm and Collected was as nervous as she was. Taylor tightened her grip.

Most of the round tables were filled with diners enjoying their meals. A few had dressed to blend with the Western decor, but the two men sitting in the red-leather-backed booth boldly stood out. Their US Navy summer white uniforms made a statement.

Shane's father's neatly clipped hair was as white as his shirt, and he was clean shaven. Three stars were displayed on his shoulder boards. Rows of service awards were proudly displayed on the left side of his shirt. The look was definitely ostentatious for the occasion. This was dinner with his son, and he could have dressed in civilian clothes.

Dane mimicked his father, but the four stripes on his shoulder boards indicated his captain status. He, too, proudly displayed his service awards on his shirt.

Shane and Dane might share the same birthday, but they had to be fraternal twins, because there wasn't much resemblance between them. Their hair was the same dark brown, but Dane's eyes were a lighter green than his brother's. Even though he was sitting down, Dane wasn't as tall as Shane, and his frame was on the smaller side.

~ 82 ~

Their waiter, dressed like a Kenny Rogers gambler complete with red garter armbands, filled their water glasses. Shane's father was the first to acknowledge them.

"Shane…" His voice trailed off when he realized his son wasn't alone. The mature gentleman's eyes did a slow sweep from Taylor's headband to her black boots. Normally, she would have called him out for the insulting inspection, but she was playing a part. Apparently, the sassy look was working.

"You didn't say you were bringing a date," his father said. "I intended for this to be a family meeting."

"Your taste in women has certainly changed." Humor laced Dane Walker's offhand compliment.

Taylor wasn't about to be put off by their rudeness. "Don't blame Shane. My plans for the evening fell through, and he asked if I'd like to meet his family." She held out her hand. "Taylor Parish, but my friends call me Tillie." She fanned her fingers to indicate the admiral should slide over. "I hope you don't mind if I sit next to you." She poured a little giddiness into her voice.

The slight twitch at the corner of Shane's mouth was the only outward sign of his amusement at the way she wasn't intimidated by his father's rudeness. His father reluctantly made room for them to slide into the booth, but kept a very polite distance between them.

"Tillie, this is my father, Harwood Walker, and my brother, Dane."

"It's nice to meet you both."

"Dad, you're looking well."

"You're looking…" He paused to take a sip of his ice water. "Like something out of an old Western movie."

"Did you park your horse out front?" Dane smiled contemptuously from the other side of the table.

What is this? Let's-beat-up-on-Shane night? His brother's smug sarcasm fired up her ire, but she managed to rein it in.

"One of the other reasons I wanted to meet with you was so we can celebrate," Harwood said. "Your brother was just promoted to the rank of captain. He's wearing four stripes on his shoulder board. If you'd stayed in the Navy, you would have already achieved that rank."

Dane tapped his own shoulder. "Navy commanders will now be reporting to me."

"Congratulations, and I still remember who reports to whom."

"You're the first admiral I've ever met," Taylor quickly said to Harwood, trying to draw the conversation away from their efforts to make Shane feel inferior.

Harwood took her comment as a way to brag about his career in the Navy. Thirty-five years and he had no plans to retire. He enjoyed his assignment in Washington, especially with his son working close by.

"And what is it you do?" Dane asked Taylor.

She moved her foot slightly and tapped Shane's boot in warning. "I write graphic novels." She'd purposely left out that the books were written for children.

"You write risqué novels?" Dane threw at her. "I'll have to look you up."

"She's amazing," Shane added. "I attended one of her private readings, and her audience hangs on every word."

Taylor rolled in her lips so she wouldn't laugh. "At my last reading, my books sold out."

The admiral gave Shane a scowl of disapproval before he returned his attention to Taylor. "How did you meet my son?"

"Shane and I are staying in the same campground. I had a problem with my motorcycle. He was able to fix it since he has the same model."

His father's back stiffened, and iciness filled his voice. "You didn't get rid of that motorcycle?" he asked Shane.

"His cycle is a honey of a ride, especially when he takes those switchbacks and pigtail turns." She was proud of herself for remembering the lingo.

"Just today, we were confronted by two bison standing in the middle of the road." Taylor purposefully batted her eyelashes at Shane. "He got us through the confrontation without anyone getting hurt."

"Gee, brother, do I hear an echo of hero worship in her praise? But then again, that's the best you can do—confront wildlife."

If Dane Walker's shin had been closer to her boot, he would've suffered a hard kick.

"Dane is a true hero," the admiral boasted. "He saved a friend when they were at Naval Academy Prep School during survival-week training. His friend was dangling from a rope, and Dane brought him up."

"My brother was there," Dane said, "but he got hurt, so I took over."

Her mad came alive when Dane gave Shane a self-righteous sneer. Something wasn't right. Shane had told her he'd saved his friend. Why wasn't he challenging his father or brother?

Her eyes darted to Shane, zeroing in on his scar. She caught the slight shake of his head, followed by the squeeze of her hand.

"Another time, they were assigned to rescue civilians in Japan after a tsunami," Harwood continued. "Two of their fellow divers got caught in debris below the surface, and he went down to save them. When he got back in the boat, a little girl was crying that her doll had gone overboard. Dane dove overboard and, through some miracle, found the doll."

"Word got back to the ship, and the press corps took a photo of me and the little girl, along with her doll. It went viral," Dane boasted.

"That's my brother, a true hero." Shane's statement dripped with sarcasm, and he gave his brother a tight-lipped grin as he lifted his water glass in a salute.

Taylor didn't know what to make of it.

Harwood leaned forward so he could address Shane directly. "Even though you're no longer wearing your uniform like your brother, I'm expecting you to be there on the Fourth to hear my speech. Dane will be there to support me."

That blowhard did it again! Why is he constantly pitting one brother against the other? It was on the tip of her tongue to ask him, but she decided not to. She didn't want to embarrass Shane or put him on the spot.

The waiter coming over to take their food order cut some of the tension, but not much. Shane barely touched his barbecue brisket. The ribs she'd ordered were delicious, but she'd be taking home a doggy bag. The other two had steak, but neither commented on how it tasted.

Her plans for the evening were definitely turning out differently than she'd expected—she had yet to learn much about the Walker family. Her biggest question was, why wouldn't Shane defend himself?

The waiter asked if anyone would like coffee. When he walked away, Dane took his cell phone out of his pocket.

"I'd like to read your books, but I can't find any under the name of Taylor Parish."

She gave him a smug smile. "That's because I don't write under that name. Try *Adventures with Tillie*."

A few moments later, his head jerked up. "These are graphic novels for kids!"

"Yes, and they're very popular, too."

"Her next two novels will have a new character—my dog, Liberty," Shane said.

"You write books for kids," Harwood confirmed. "Why didn't you say so in the first place?"

Taylor aimed her response directly at Harwood. "Things aren't always what they appear. I also teach history and social studies to middle-school children. Sometimes you have to look a little deeper to get beyond prejudices and see the truth."

His response was just what she anticipated: He gave her a blank stare and remained silent.

She wasn't done and nodded at Dane. "Wearing that uniform makes a statement, but it's what's inside that makes a true hero."

His complexion turned pale, but like his father, he remained silent.

*****

Dinner was exactly what he'd expected it to be—beat-up-on-Shane time. Over the years, his shoulders had carried the weight of his father's put-downs. The load had gotten worse since he'd retired. He was aware of his brother's promotion and had anticipated his gloating. At his bachelor party, Benny had told Shane that Harwood's influence had helped push the promotion through.

Little did they realize that if Shane had stayed in the Navy, he would've been promoted to captain, and his brother would have reported to Shane. No, nothing could make Dane look inferior.

Taylor was doing a great job of running blocker. Actually, she'd gone above and beyond and quickly read into his family. *Things aren't always what they seem. Sometimes you have to look a little deeper to get beyond prejudices and see the truth.*

He'd told her the truth about how he got his scar, but he'd left out a lot of the details. He'd better be prepared to answer her questions about his brother's "hero status."

"So I'll expect you to be at my speech," his father said, drawing Shane's attention.

What he was about to ask would surely raise his father's ire, but he didn't have to hold back any longer. "That depends. Will your speech be all about you, or will you include the military legacy the Walker family has carried on since the Revolutionary War?"

His father's reddened cheeks preceded his blustering. "I'm a three-star admiral! Remember to whom you're talking!"

"Since I'm no longer in the Navy and don't report to you, I'm talking to my father."

"Admiral, don't worry," Dane said, "I'll be there to support you."

"Thank you, Dane. I can always depend on you to show me the respect I deserve."

This irritating family reunion had gone on long enough. Shane squeezed Taylor's hand before he stood. "Dad, Dane, it was good seeing you both. If you're not busy tomorrow, why don't you check out the Lincoln Borglum Museum to find out about the history of Mount Rushmore? It will be more meaningful when you give your speech."

"Shane, considering you're on a pension, I'll take care of the bill." Dane snickered.

Taylor rose. "It was a pleasure meeting you. Shane is correct. It's the true heroes who aren't talked about—for example, the miners who blasted and dug the rock."

He put a firm hand to Taylor's elbow to guide her away from them before she could start lecturing his family about heroes. He didn't need a first-row seat in her mind to know what was coming.

He'd no sooner started the truck and backed out of the parking space before his cab was filled with Taylor expelling her simmering temper.

"What in God's name was going on back there? You saved your friend and have a scar to prove it! I don't know who I'm angrier with. You or your father and brother! How can you be so calm after being subjected to such a put-down? Why didn't you defend yourself?"

He stopped at a traffic light, and his fist came down hard on the wheel. "You think I'm not angry?" he spewed. "I've had to put up with that sh—" He caught himself. "Crap all my life. Harwood is my father, but he never let me forget he was my superior. 'This is your lieutenant commander talking to you, boy!' I was only seven-years-old!" He sighed heavily. "I'm sorry, Taylor."

A warm hand touched the backs of his fingers that gripped the steering wheel. "I told you my shoulders were strong. When we get back to the campground, let's get out of these clothes. The tightness of this bustier is making it hard to breathe.

Then I'll make us some hot chocolate with marshmallows. We can snack on chocolate chip cookies, since our dinner companions took our appetites away."

"You went above and beyond the call of duty, and I'm not just talking about your sexy top. Thanks again for going with me, and I'll apologize again for my father's rude behavior. You were clever and very astute when you said, 'Things aren't always what they seem. Sometimes you have to look a little deeper to get beyond prejudices and see the truth.' You were referring to my brother's claim he saved my buddy Benny."

"It's apparent your father is unaware of a lot of things. How long have you been covering for Dane?"

"Since we were kids. Be forewarned, your shoulders will definitely be bent when I get finished with my tale about the Walker twins."

Chapter 8

"This is your last cookie!" Shane tossed a dog biscuit to Liberty, who'd made herself comfortable on Taylor's couch. Winnie sprawled across the back, keeping an eye on the goings-on. Drinking hot chocolate and eating cookies with Taylor was just what Shane had needed to bring him back to his happy place. The short time he'd spent with his family had convinced him retiring was the best decision he'd ever made.

The other best decision was pursuing Taylor Parish. Like a well-trained halfback, she'd stepped in to take the heat off from his father's attack.

Liberty had barked as soon as he'd parked the truck, and he'd taken her for a walk before he'd changed his clothes. The shorts and T-shirt were a lot more comfortable than his Western outfit had been.

"Your sexy-biker look was great, but now you look like yourself." The red bandanna she'd used as a headband was wrapped around her ponytail. "Thanks again for going with me."

"I'm a T-shirt-and-jeans kind of girl." She held up her foot. "Moccasins, too. I'm ready to listen to the story about the Walker twins."

"I was born first and weighed a pound more than my brother. He had breathing problems, and they kept him in the hospital longer. He also had to gain more weight. While we were growing up, my mother and father babied him, more or less keeping him in a protective bubble. If I had something, and he wanted it, he'd start to cry. My mother would tell me to give it to him."

"You've never mentioned your mother before."

"Fifteen years ago, she walked out on my dad. Her note said she was tired of being told how to be the perfect wife of a naval officer. She needed to make a life of her own. A friend of hers let us know she got a job working in an antique shop in a small town in Pennsylvania. She was happy, but later was diagnosed with pancreatic cancer. She died peacefully. Well, as peacefully as someone can with cancer."

"I'm sorry, Shane. So tell me about more about your brother."

"Dane learned quickly how to always get his way. He'd break something and claim I did it. While I was getting hollered at, he'd stand behind our parents and laugh and stick his tongue out at me, knowing they'd never holler at him because he was too frail."

"That sucks! What a spoiled brat! Was he really not healthy?"

"I was stronger, but we were both healthy. He is slightly smaller than me. You have no idea what it's like to be constantly badgered, 'You're the older one and have to look out for your brother.' This continued through adulthood."

"That's the reason you didn't defend yourself at dinner tonight. Have you ever tried to tell your father the truth, like about how you're the one who saved Benny?"

"Even as a kid, I realized I would be wasting my breath. I know what I did. It gave me personal satisfaction knowing I saved my friend."

"Why hasn't Benny ever set the record straight?"

"Benny was so out of it when I got him topside, he wasn't able to back me up later. I'd no sooner gotten him settled than the world around me started to spin, and I passed out. I woke up in the ER. One of the instructors from the academy came in to see how I was doing. He let me know that my brother was a hero, having saved Benny and me."

Taylor shook her head. "Dane has got a major ego problem. How was he able to survive in the Navy without you?"

Shane snickered, barely able to hold in a laugh. "My father used his influence to ensure we were in the same unit, just in case."

"What did you do when you were in the Navy?"

"I was a Navy fleet diver. They perform underwater salvage, repair and maintenance, submarine rescue. We support special warfare and explosive ordinance disposal."

"You handled explosives?"

"Not all ordinances explode during a war. Divers will find intact torpedoes, and we remove them."

"It sounds fascinating and dangerous. Before you retired, where were you stationed?"

"Panama City, Florida. The US Navy Experimental Diving Unit is located there. The unit is composed of a hundred twenty service personnel drawn from numerous components of the Navy. I was also part of the Naval Support Activity. It's the largest diving facility in the world. It's their job to execute the US military's special diving tasks, like saturation diving."

Taylor dipped her head to the side. "What is saturation diving?"

He gave her a tolerant smile. "A diver remains underwater at a certain depth, breathing a mixture of gasses under pressure for an indefinite period. It allows the diver to work at great depths and reduces the total time spent undergoing decompression."

"Your brother's a diver, too?"

Shane nodded. "When I let it be known I was retiring, my father found my brother a nice, safe desk job at the Navy Public Affairs Office in Washington." Taylor was easy to talk to, and it felt good getting a lot of angst off his chest. He helped himself to another cookie.

"I'm sorry, Shane, truly sorry your family has treated you so unfairly. Do you miss living in Florida and diving?"

"I loved my job, but it was time to retire. As for diving, I do it for pleasure now." He glanced at the time on her microwave. "It's getting late. I don't know what your plans are for tomorrow, but I'm heading for the Crazy Horse Memorial. Care to join me? If you can stand my company, that is?"

"Shane, you're the best time I've ever had researching for my next book."

"I don't think I've ever been anyone's best time." *Taylor Parish, where have you been all my life?*

"I'd love to join you tomorrow, but I was hoping to explore Mount Rushmore."

"I thought you wanted to go to the nighttime program?"

"I want to do that, too, but you can see more of the monument during the day."

He, too, wanted to see Mount Rushmore up close. If he went during the day, he wouldn't have to go to the evening show on the Fourth and listen to his father. "If we leave early enough, we can we visit both attractions. What time do you want to leave?"

"Around nine o'clock. I'll even pack our lunch."

Shane finished the rest of his coffee and stood up. "Come on, Ms. Liberty. One more walk tonight, then it's beddy-bye."

Taylor also rose. Shane took hold of her hand and pressed a kiss on the backs of her knuckles, wishing they were her soft lips. "Thanks for putting up with my rude, eccentric family and letting me vent."

"When you think about it, you're a true hero for putting up with those bubbleheads!"

"Taylor, I'm not a hero. See you in the morning."

*****

Taylor adjusted the strap on the seat belt that ran across her chest. They'd left for the trip to Crazy Horse Memorial a little while ago. Sitting in the cup holders between the seats were two insulated containers of ice water. The drive was supposed to take only twenty minutes, but they'd already encountered a traffic backup as soon as they passed through the small town of Custer. The terrain soon changed to tree-covered mountains.

Taylor did a quick read through the brochure she'd picked up at the campground. "I should've read through this before I suggested we go to both monuments in one day." She looked up when Shane applied the brakes. "You must be a magnet for wildlife."

A bighorn sheep was standing in the middle of the road. The bold creature twisted his head around, showing off his impressive, curved horns.

"At this rate, we'll get to the attraction by late afternoon."

"Remember, this is their land, and we're just visitors," she said with a laugh. "The entry fee to Crazy Horse is fifteen dollars for each person. The monument itself is a distance from the Welcome Center, so if we want to get a closer look, we can pay four dollars to take a bus for a twenty-five-minute round-trip tour where we'll be able to get out to get a closer view of the faces. They're currently working on Crazy Horse's left hand and the horse's mane. Once it's finished, it will be 563 feet high and 641 feet wide."

He glanced at her from the corner of his eye. "It's the world's largest mountain carving. The head alone is twenty-seven feet taller than any of the heads at Mount Rushmore."

"If I were your teacher, I'd give you extra points for doing your homework. What else did you learn?"

"They started on the monument in 1948."

"That's seventy-four years ago!"

"They don't expect to finish it until 2050 or later," he added. The sheep fueled his ego for the moment and meandered across the highway. Shane sighed with relief and put the truck in drive. "The project is privately funded by a nonprofit organization. No government funding is provided."

"Now we know where the entry fees are going."

A few minutes later, they turned onto Avenue of the Chiefs, which led to the parking lot across from the Welcome Center. Midmorning had brought out a lot of tourists, and they were lucky to find a parking space.

The line to pay the entry fee moved slowly with so many visitors, including young families with strollers. The temperature was eighty degrees, but felt hotter without a breeze.

Taylor removed her credit card and returned her wallet to her hip purse. "I'm paying since you won't let me pay for gas."

"Deal, but dinner is on me. I hope you like Mexican."

"You're cooking?"

"No." He laughed. "There's an authentic Mexican restaurant in Custer. I ate there the other night, and the food was great." He tapped her on the shoulder. "The line is moving."

Two reservations on the sightseeing van had been canceled, so they were lucky to get seats on it. Shane gave Taylor the window seat.

The driver had barely pulled away from the Welcome Center when he tapped on a microphone, drawing their attention. "Crazy Horse was an Oglala Sioux Indian chief who fought against the government that was taking the land and changing the way of life for Native Americans. He also fought alongside Chief Sitting Bull in the Battle of the Little Bighorn."

"Also known as Custer's Last Stand," Shane quietly added.

"The elevation of Crazy Horse Memorial is 6,532 feet above sea level, and it ranks as the twenty-seventh-highest mountain in South Dakota. Make sure you watch the movie at the Welcome Center."

A tourist seated up front asked, "What's it made of?"

"Sculptor Korczak Ziolkowski and Lakota Chief Henry Standing Bear chose pegmatite granite. Although they haven't been sculpted yet, when complete, the horse's head will be 219 feet high, the horse's mane will be sixty-two feet high, the ears will be fifty-four feet long, the eyes will be twenty feet wide and fifteen feet high, and his nose will be twenty-six foot in diameter."

Taylor nudged Shane's shoulder. "I'll bet you didn't know the horse's dimensions."

"No, I didn't." He nudged her shoulder in return. "I'll bet you don't know the name of his horse."

"No, smart guy, I don't, but I'm sure you're going to tell me," she teased right back.

"A medicine man named Horn Chips gave the chief a black stone to protect the pinto he named Inyan, which means rock or stone. He placed the stone behind the black-and-white horse's ear, so they'd become one in battle."

Taylor leaned back and gave him an appreciative stare. "You would make a great teacher."

His smile disappeared, and he shifted his gaze toward the front of the bus. Their shoulders touched when the bus made a wide turn. "That's what I always wanted to do, work with young children and teach."

"I'm not going to ask why you didn't, since I already figured it out. Your brother wanted to go into the Navy, so your father determined that's what you had to do, too."

"You're right. I'm not saying I didn't enjoy my time in the Navy. It was a great experience, and I loved serving my country. The guys I trained and worked with are lifelong friends. We had a few close calls, but any one of us would have given his life for the others."

True heroes. Too bad she couldn't say what she was thinking.

A hot breeze caught the end of her ponytail and brushed it against her cheek when she got out of the bus. They joined other tourists who wanted to get a closer view of the monument in progress. Workers had roped off the area to keep tourists in the safety zone.

Talk about overwhelming. The edifice was magnificent. The detail in the unsmiling face was majestic. The cracks in the warrior's face were evident from having had to endure many years of the sun's intense rays. It boasted of power and strength, as if to say, *I can't be beaten!*

A warm tear slid down her cheek, and she brushed it away with back of her hand.

"Why are you crying?"

She blinked back more tears and shrugged a shoulder. "This proud chief defended his people. The government took his land, but he fought back and won. He's a guardian, looking over the Black Hills, his land, and he will do so for thousands of years."

His hand slipped into hers. "Many people will just stare and think, 'What a big rock sculpture,' but you've seen what the sculptor wants people to see. Taylor, you're amazing."

It wasn't the heat of the day that made her cheeks feel hot. For someone she'd just met, Shane understood her, and he hadn't said she was silly for crying.

The bus driver signaled everyone to get back to the van for the return trip to the Welcome Center.

"When we get back, we should have lunch and then watch the documentary about the history of the monument," Taylor suggested.

"Don't forget there are three museums and a gift shop. Now I'm glad we decided to visit only one attraction today."

Taylor squeezed his hand slightly. "Thanks for being such a great tour buddy. I usually have to do this alone, but it's nice to be able to share it with you. If I become annoying, and you don't want to do something, let me know."

"You mean if you become a PITA?" he returned with a wink. "I won't be afraid to speak up."

Taylor was even more appreciative of Shane's patience when she took her time going through the museums. She made note after note, on the Crazy Horse Memorial. Many of the other tourists had left by the time they walked back to his truck late in the afternoon.

"I'll be the first to admit I never expected to see such an overwhelming exhibit, the museums, and the film. Tillie is going to have to have a separate book about the Crazy Horse Memorial." She sighed, took a long drink of cold water and relaxed against the back of the seat. "I don't know if you saw the sign, but they have a light show nightly."

"I'm sure it's awesome and will be packed, considering it's the Fourth of July weekend."

"I agree." She didn't bring up the fireworks at the end of the Independence Day show at Mount Rushmore. "Getting there will definitely be a challenge."

"I'm ready for some great Mexican food. We can either do takeout or eat it there."

"Let's get the full Mexican experience and eat in."

The restaurant was part of a small strip mall. From the amount of people sitting at the tables and standing in line to place their orders, the Mexican food here had to be delicious. Taylor looked about, noting the pictures of the owners' Mexican heritage displayed on the painted brown, gold, and red walls.

They stood back and read the menu posted on the wall behind the two girls who were taking orders at the front counter.

"Shane, what's the difference between a burrito and a chimichanga?"

"If your burrito is fried, then it's a chimichanga. It's served on a plate. A burrito is hand-rolled, wrapped in foil, and you can eat it with your hands."

"Since you've eaten here before, what do you recommend?"

"The quesadillas are great, and so are the fajita burritos. I'm going to have two pork tamales and the beef chimichanga. We can share an order of cheese nachos and salsa."

"I'm going to try a chimichanga with a side of refried beans and rice."

Once they placed their order, the girl said she'd call Shane's name when it was ready for pickup. Taylor turned and spotted a couple vacating a booth. "Let's commandeer the soft seats."

Before sitting down, they got their drinks from a soda machine. She leaned back against the brown leather seat and couldn't erase the smile from her face. "Shane Walker, like I said, you are the best time I've ever had. Today was a lot more fun because I got to share it with you."

"Taylor Parish, I ditto your sentiment. When do you plan to visit Mount Rushmore?"

"It's on my agenda for tomorrow."

Before he could reply, his cell phone pinged with an incoming text. The scowl faded, replaced by a big smile. "Three of my buddies are in town for the celebration and want to meet up with me tomorrow. They're part of the Blue Angels that will be doing a flyover before the sun sets. They're at Ellsworth Air Force Base." He paused to call up a maps app on his phone. "Box Elder is only a forty-five-minute drive from here. Wait a minute. That would leave you without transportation tomorrow."

"Don't worry about it. I've got plenty of writing to do."

"If you want to drive my truck, I'll take my cycle. I wouldn't mind riding the Needles Highway again."

Her momentary disappointment was replaced by excitement. "If you don't mind, neither do I."

"I'll leave a little after nine, but will bring you the keys before then. I'm sure I won't be home until tomorrow evening. Would you take Liberty for a couple of walks?"

"It's the least I can do."

A few minutes later, Shane's name was called, and he walked up to the counter to get their food. He'd been right. It was some of the best Mexican food she'd ever eaten.

Chapter 9

    A little after nine o'clock the following morning, Shane delivered the keys to his truck and a spare key to his trailer. To her delight, he was wearing his Western outfit, but had covered the rawhide vest with his black leather jacket. The anticipation of meeting his friends was evident in his big smile. She hoped he'd share a little about his association with his buddies after their visit.

    Before hurrying off, he said if she had any problems, she should text him. The thoughtful concern for her welfare was very much appreciated. Having lived alone since Aunt Tillie had passed away, she'd had no one to depend upon but herself. Back home, her teacher friends were available if she had any problems. In a very short time, Shane had become so special to her.

    A grim reminder was that she'd be moving on after the July Fourth celebration, leaving Shane. Too soon, much too soon. She hoped to persuade him to visit Philadelphia with her. She'd stress the importance of Liberty being there when she started the story line for the next book. Before suggesting he visit the City of Brotherly Love, she had to find a way to get him to attend the festivities at Mount Rushmore tomorrow night.

She continued to ignore the repeated messages coming from her conscience. *Are you doing the right thing by pushing him to attend the nighttime show?*

Driving Shane's truck was fun, considering it was so much smaller than her bus. With America's birthday the following day, Mount Rushmore had drawn a larger-than-normal crowd. When she walked down the Avenue of Flags, she felt surrounded by history and paused to admire the array of colorful flags fluttering in the early morning breeze. From her research, she knew the Avenue of Flags had been established for the US Bicentennial in 1976. A familiar voice behind her was delivering more information, and she turned toward the man.

"The fifty-six flags represent the fifty states, the District of Columbia, the three territories and the two commonwealths of the United States. The monument was the vision of sculptor Gutzon Borglum. It took fourteen years to complete. From 1927 to 1941, men and women worked to blast and carve the faces of Presidents George Washington, Thomas Jefferson, Theodore Roosevelt, and Abraham Lincoln."

The smile that filled her face couldn't have gotten any bigger. Luis Cabrera, an interpretive park ranger, was speaking to a woman dressed in tan and brown military camo. He took pride in wearing his standard green and gunmetal shirt and iconic broad-brimmed flat hat. She'd had the pleasure of working with him at the Delaware Water Gap National Recreation Area a number of years ago. The last time they'd communicated, he'd let her know he'd been transferred to Castillo de San Marcos National Monument in St. Augustine, Florida.

She took a few steps in his direction, and his eyes opened wide in recognition. "They'll let anyone in this place," he said with a smile.

"Luis, I can't believe you're here!" They shared a big hug. "Are you based here now?"

"No," he said, shaking his head. "I'm only here for a couple of weeks, and then it's back to Florida. Pardon me, this is Petty Officer Second Class Midori Sato. She's part of a special Navy contingent brought in for the Fourth of July celebration tomorrow night. We're expecting a big crowd."

"I'm pleased to meet you, Midori. Thank you for your service."

"You're welcome, and it's a pleasure to meet you, too."

"Midori, Taylor Parish writes graphic novels for middle-school children. She makes learning history much more fun."

"I try. Midori, you've picked the perfect interpretive ranger to talk to. Luis is a fount of information about national parks. Any chance I can tag along for a little while?"

His answer was just a grin before they headed for the Presidential Trail. Even though she'd walked the half-mile trail with Shane, she enjoyed doing it again with Luis while he gave his informative talk. She also didn't mind traversing the 422 stairs that brought her closer to the monument. A number of times, Luis was approached by tourists with questions. Their little group expanded to a dozen.

He stopped the group and asked if anyone had any questions. When everyone held back, he looked at Taylor. "We have a guest with us. She writes *Adventures with Tillie*, historical fiction books for middle-school children."

One of the children in the front of the group raised her hand. "I love those books, especially Winnemucca!"

"Ms. Taylor, would you like to share with everyone something you've found unique in your research?" Luis asked.

"I certainly would." She switched into teacher mode. "How many of you know there's a secret room in the monument?"

"Oh, you mean like in that movie *National Treasure*," one of the adults commented. "That stuff's all in the movies."

She looked at Luis and winked. "I can assure you it's true. There's a secret room in Abraham Lincoln's section of the mountain. The sculptor of Mount Rushmore designed it. You're probably wondering why. The space was designed to preserve things that showed the entire history of America, including the Bill of Rights, the Constitution, the Declaration of Independence, and a lot more."

She took a deep breath when Luis added a little more information. "President Roosevelt earned his place on the monument because he was a firm believer in preserving the natural resources of our country. He contributed to the creation of the secret room, but he died before being able to complete the history of America, but others took over."

"When can we go there?", a young boy asked.

"There aren't any tours since the door is actually on Abraham Lincoln's face, so we can't just go up there to get in."

"Rumor has it there was supposed to be a fifth face sculpted. What happened?" a woman at the back of the group asked.

Taylor smiled, and gave a brief story of Susan B. Anthony.

Two hours later, Luis had a lunch break and asked if she and Midori would like to join him in the Carvers' Café. They all had Italian subs, and she insisted on treating her friends.

"Midori, I hope you don't mind answering this question, but what made you join the Navy?"

"I don't mind at all. Would you believe a hero, though I don't even know his name."

Taylor was immediately intrigued. "I'd love to hear the rest of your story."

"When I was ten years old, my family and I were visiting my grandparents in the Tohoku region of Japan. They grow rice there."

Taylor's mind automatically jumped to the article she'd read about Dane Walker saving a little girl. *Is this a coincidence or what? Get your facts straight.* "Tell me you weren't there for that devastating earthquake that caused the tsunami."

~ 110 ~

Midori nodded at Taylor. "We were, and I occasionally still have nightmares about it."

The watery film covering the young woman's eyes said this would be painful to talk about. Taylor touched the back of the young petty officer's hand. "If it's too upsetting, you don't have to tell me."

"No, it's okay. I want you to know. The entire coastline was swept away. It also instigated a major nuclear accident at a power station along the coast. Navy helicopters were deployed to help search and rescue. We were in the water, and Navy divers in rigid inflatable boats rescued as many of us as they could. Their efforts were challenged by the offshore debris field, which was unbelievable.

"We were in one of the boats. Two divers saved my grandparents' neighbors and got them into another boat. Before the divers could get out of the water, a strong wave took them under. When they didn't come up, one of the divers on our boat dove into the water. They were down for quite a while. Then three heads appeared. I later found out the two divers had gotten trapped by debris. The boat was full, so he returned to us."

"So that made you want to join the Navy?" Luis asked.

"No, there's more. No matter where I went, I always brought along a doll I got when I was three years old. Sakura—her name means cherry blossoms—was in my arms. A wave rocked the boat so much, she went overboard and started to sink. The sailor who rescued the two drivers went back into the water to look for my doll."

"So he found it?"

She nodded at Luis. "Yes. One of the other divers, who stayed in our boat the whole time, grabbed a rescue blanket, and wrapped it around me and my doll. They took us back to their ship, and he carried me aboard. People started taking pictures of me in the sailor's arms. They were interested in the humanitarian side of the rescue."

Bells from a five-alarm fire were going off in Taylor's head. Midori *was* the little girl Dane Walker claimed to have rescued, but something was definitely off.

"Midori, do you know the name of the diver who rescued you?"

"Not his first name, but his last name is Walker. I've since learned there are two brothers named Walker, and their father is an admiral. He'll be giving a speech here tomorrow night."

"Where are you currently stationed?"

"The US Navy Experimental Diving Unit in Panama City, Florida."

"A friend of mine was stationed there until he retired from the Navy six months ago. Shane Walker."

"I was just transferred there."

The puzzle pieces were falling into place, but she couldn't complete the picture without getting a few more pieces of information. "Do you know what happened to the sailor who saved your doll? Not the diver who wrapped you in a blanket and took all the credit, but the man who went in after your doll."

"No. He gave me my doll and swam to the other boat to check on the two divers he saved. When we got to the ship, my parents were with me, but they were too upset to answer any questions. I do remember one of the men asking me if the sailor who held me was the one who saved me. All I did was crush my doll to my face."

"That was a harrowing experience, and I'm so glad you and your family were saved. Do you by any chance still have the doll?"

"As a matter of fact, I do. I consider her my good luck charm. She never leaves my travel duffel."

"Taylor, why are you asking all these questions?" Luis asked.

"Luis, a great miscarriage of justice has been made. How much influence do you have over the program that's going to take place tomorrow evening?"

"I'm the master of ceremonies. I'll be giving a welcoming speech and a small informational talk about Mount Rushmore and showing a short film on the history of the presidents. We've got the US Air Force Band playing patriotic songs. After intermission, Admiral Walker will give his speech. Then I'll ask all military personnel, active and retired, to come down onto the stage. Each will be asked to give his or her name and branch of service. Taps will be played while we lower the flag, and then there'll be fireworks."

She looked first at Midori and then Luis. "If at all possible, could you insert a special addition to the program, right before you invite all military personnel to the stage?"

"I need a little more information," Luis pressed.

She gave Midori a tender smile. "I know the real sailor who saved you and those two divers. Do you think you can bring your doll tomorrow night?"

"Sure, but tell me more. I'd like to thank him personally."

"This is what I'd like you to do."

She exchanged cell phone numbers with her coconspirators. Luis would let her know if he'd be able to add an additional short speech to the program. Taylor would see them tomorrow night. Before heading back to the campground, she paused to admire the flags blowing in the afternoon breeze, appreciating what they represented.

On her way back to Shane's truck, her conscience sent a little stronger message. *Shane is going to be angry with you for your conniving. You just met the man, and you're making life-changing decisions for him! And you thought to invite him to go to Philadelphia with you. That certainly won't happen after this.*

Before she could tell her conscience to MYOB, she spied another familiar face, this one not very welcome. Dane Walker, and he wasn't alone.

His companion was an attractive woman who appeared to be in her early thirties. Her long blond hair was caught at the back of her neck with a red barrette. Wedge sandals brought her head above Dane's shoulders. Her white capris were as white as Dane's summer dress uniform. A red-white-and-blue-striped scarf dressed up her red short-sleeve blouse.

All Taylor could think when she looked at them was Patriotic Barbie and Ken.

"Ms. Parish, so nice to see you again."

The sarcasm she'd associated with Dane Walker wasn't there. Who was he trying to impress? *Taylor, there's a guy behind them carrying a camera.*

"Dane. Fancy meeting you here. You're a day early to stand in the spotlight."

His right hand curled into a fist, letting her know she'd hit a sore spot. "Courtney Altman, I'd like you to meet Taylor Parish. She authors graphic novels for middle-school children called *Adventures with Tillie*."

"It's a pleasure to meet you." Her red lips curved in a smile. "I'm familiar with your book series. My nephew has all of them, and he's learned to love history."

"I'm glad he enjoys them. Taking a tour of the monument?"

"As you know, I'm in public affairs," Dane said. "Ms. Altman is a reporter from Trent Media who is covering the event. I'm giving her an interview about the Walker family."

Yeah, a bunch of lies. She raised a brow. "I'm sure you're going to include your heroic past, too."

He responded to zinger number two by making a fist with his left hand and stiffening his back. "The Walkers have served this country since the

Revolutionary War, and heroism is part of who we are."

The anger she'd experienced the other night was back, but this wasn't the time or place to cause a scene. Come tomorrow night…

"It was very nice meeting you, Ms. Altman. Word of advice: Make sure you confirm all of your facts before you publish your article."

When she headed toward the truck, she didn't need eyes in the back of her head to see the fire of resentment in Dane Walker's gaze.

She got back to the campground a little after four o'clock. The first thing she did was take Liberty for a walk, after getting lots of kisses first. Only two other pet owners were sitting on benches in the dog park. One was an older gentleman with a beagle and a Jack Russell terrier, the other a teenage girl who was working with her collie going up and down the ramps.

Liberty did her business before joining the other two dogs. Taylor sat beside the gentleman on the bench. He introduced himself and let her know he recognized Liberty, having met her owner earlier. The Vietnam veteran emblem on the gentleman's hat drew her attention.

When she said, "Thank you for your service," he explained he came to Mount Rushmore every Fourth of July so he could represent his fellow servicemen who'd never made it home.

An hour later, she returned to her trailer, hoping she'd made the right decision in asking Luis and Midori to arrange the additional presentation. Dane was a coward and a glory hound.

She sat at her computer and revisited the article she'd read on the 2011 earthquake and tsunami in the Tohoku region of Japan. This time, she clicked on an additional link that took her to the humanitarian efforts in the area from all over the world. The pictures included in the article showed the gut-wrenching devastation the tsunami had caused.

Her stomach turned a little more. A photo showed the rat fink holding Midori and her doll in his arms. In the accompanying story, he related the rescues of the little girl and the two Navy divers. He took credit for that, too!

One of the divers was Benny Acosta, the same guy Shane had rescued when they were in Naval Academy Prep School. Shane had mentioned Benny's recent wedding had taken place in Rapid City. An idea sparked to life. The hometown boy had gone to Annapolis, so there might be other articles about him. Her fingers flew across the keys.

A little while later, she shut down the computer, wearing a big smile. If she could get Benny to show up, it would further support her campaign to convince Shane it was okay to be a hero.

*****

What a great day! Spending time with Kevin, Brian and Sean had made Shane appreciate the importance of lifelong friends. As they were stationed in Pensacola, Florida, during the summer months, he had been able to see them more often when he was stationed in Florida, too.

They'd been eager to hear what Shane had been doing since he'd retired. When they'd asked what he wanted to do with himself, he couldn't give them an answer. Right now, he was having fun traveling around the country. He hadn't been surprised when they'd asked if there was anyone "special" in his life. He'd brightened up and told them about Taylor, her books, and her plans to make Liberty a new character.

Neither his father nor brother were mentioned. He'd promised to let them know what he decided to do and how his "relationship" with Taylor Parish went.

The surprise he'd had when he'd walked into his trailer a little while ago was an added bonus. Not that Liberty wasn't happy to see him, based on the amount of doggy kisses he'd received.

The surprise was a note on the counter attached to a Ziploc bag filled with homemade chocolate chip cookies.

Welcome home! I missed you today! Thanks again for letting me borrow your truck. I hope you had a great time with your friends. Looking forward to hearing all about it. Liberty was a good girl and played nice with the other dogs. Keys to your truck and trailer on the counter. I'm having pancakes in the event center at nine o'clock. Hope to see you there.

He immediately looked out the window to see if there were any lights on in Taylor's bus, but it was dark. He'd thank her in the morning.

~ 118 ~

Shane ate two cookies and took a few swigs of milk right from the bottle before he attached the leash to Liberty's collar and headed for the doggy park.

He breathed in the nighttime air, catching the hint of burning logs. The temperature had dropped to sixty degrees, inviting campers to build fires in the fire pits that were part of each campsite. Many of the campers had attached red, white, and blue lights to their awnings, along with triangular banners of the American flag.

Just before he got to the doggy park, he stopped to watch three children holding sparklers, swirling them around and laughing with glee. Their parents stood right beside them, already prepared for the next round.

It made him feel downhearted. His father had never shared any type of happy, simple moments with him and his brother. He doubted his father remembered their birth date. Harwood never dropped the ball when either of his sons was promoted. He expected loyalty at all times, so why should Shane support his father tomorrow night?

Liberty tugged harder on her leash, recognizing the fenced-in enclosure. "Okay, you've been cooped up all day." He opened the gate, removed the leash, and the dog took off, joining the two dogs Shane recognized. He walked over to the bench and sat down.

"Evening, Mr. Berweiler. How are you doing?"

The older gentleman sighed deeply. "Not good. I wanted to go into town this morning, but my truck wouldn't start. There's a problem with the alternator. Won't hold a charge."

"I'm sorry to hear that. I'm pretty good with engines. Do you want me to take a look at it tomorrow?"

The veteran put a hand to Shane's shoulder. "I appreciate the offer, but I ran a service garage for forty years, so I know engines. I called the auto-parts store in Deadwood, and they have to order it. The new alternator will be here in three days."

"If you need anything in town, I'll be glad to take you."

"No, thanks. I'm good foodwise for me and the dogs. I can also eat at the luncheonette. I'm more upset because I won't be able to go to the Fourth of July celebration at Mount Rushmore. I tried to see if there were any seats left on the buses they use to take campers to the monument to alleviate the overcrowded parking. They're all sold out, and there's a waiting list."

He sighed again. "If I don't go, I'll be letting down my fellow countrymen who gave their lives for this country in Vietnam. Some of my buddies never made it home. I also recently found out I'm the only one left from our unit."

Shane recalled what he'd thought earlier. His father didn't deserve his loyalty. Here was a gentleman who had served his country and wasn't looking for a pat on the back or to be referred to as a hero. All he wanted to do was support his fellow countrymen.

Shane stood up and held out a hand. "I wasn't planning to go, but I'll be happy to take you to the ceremony. I'm just warning you. My father is going to give a speech. If you see me walk away, I'm not leaving. I'll bring you home after the fireworks."

The strength in the older gentleman's grip was surprising. "I'd be honored if you'd stand beside me when they invite all military personnel to come down to the stage. Remember what I said the first time we met? It's not about you. You'd be honoring the men and women you served with."

The passion and determination in Sergeant Berweiler's voice struck an inner chord. He wasn't his father or brother, who needed outward recognition. Shane had honorably served his country and would do so again if he got called up. Courage didn't automatically make him or anyone else a hero. He'd proudly stand beside the retired Vietnam veteran.

Chapter 10

The old saying *nervous as a cat in a room full of rocking chairs* fit Taylor perfectly. How she'd gotten through the day without giving away what was supposed to happen in a little while she'd never know. This morning at breakfast, Shane had arrived just as she'd gotten in line. He'd greeted her with a big smile, a quick hug, and a kiss on the cheek. They'd just sat down at the table when Mr. Berweiler had asked if he could sit with them.

Shane had started to make the introductions when she let him know that she'd met the Vietnam vet the day before. She'd hidden her reaction when he'd also let her know he'd be taking the sergeant to Mount Rushmore for the evening show, explaining the problem with the older gentleman's truck. He'd invited her to ride to the event with them.

As soon as they'd finished breakfast, she'd gone over to the reception center and had their names removed from the bus list.

Shane's good mood continued when he related his visit with his three friends, who were Blue Angels. Mr. Berweiler said how much he admired the pilots and wondered how the pilots kept from passing out from flying at such high altitudes.

Shane explained his friends trained and performed seven or eight-g maneuvers routinely. During the anti-g straining maneuver, the pilots made a hick-sounding grunt close to the glottis, behind the Adam's apple. The maneuver helped control the flow of blood and prevented passing out.

She'd asked if he'd ever tried it, and he'd laughed out loud, claiming his friends were crazier than he was.

Now, as anticipated, all 2,500 seats in the amphitheater were filled. A flurry of American flags in the hands of the spectators filled the night air. Children wore headbands with blinking red, white and blue stars.

When they'd gotten seated, she'd purposely suggested the men sit at the end of the row close to the stairway. Along with his signature Vietnam vet cap, the retired Air Force sergeant wore a regulation light blue dress shirt with his rank insignia proudly displayed on the short sleeves. She, too, had opted to be patriotic and wore a red short-sleeved blouse, white shorts, and navy-blue sneakers.

They were enjoying a half-hour intermission. Luis had texted her a final copy of the program she wasn't to share with anyone. He'd gotten the okay to have Midori Sato come out onstage and give a brief talk. Harwood would be starting off the second half. After the petty officer's brief address, all the servicemen and servicewomen would be invited to come down to the stage for the same ending he'd told her about yesterday.

She checked her watch and figured they had another fifteen minutes before the intermission was over. "I'm going to the ladies' room. Be right back."

Of course she'd pick the time everyone wanted to hit the restroom. The line was long, but went a lot quicker than she anticipated. When she was washing her hands, she looked in the mirror and noticed the woman three sinks away was Courtney Altman, the reporter from Trent Media. Once again, she was decked out in her red, white, and blue finery. As soon as they exited the building, the woman approached Taylor.

"Ms. Parish, do you have a minute?"

"Sure, what can I do for you?"

"What did you mean yesterday when you said I should be sure to check my facts before writing my story?"

Not knowing what Dane Walker had told the woman, she couldn't come out and say he was a liar. She decided to steer the woman in another direction. "I know you're here to write a story on the Fourth of July celebration, but I've got a human-interest angle that will make your article shine."

"So tell me!"

"I can't. It's not my story to tell, but be sure to have your cameraman ready after Admiral Walker's speech. Now, if you'll excuse me, I've got to get back to my seat before intermission is over." When her conscience remained quiet, she figured she was doing the right thing.

"That was quick. Usually, the line to the ladies' room is a mile long," Shane teased her as she was sitting down.

"Funny, Shane Walker," she said. "What do you think of the show so far?"

"It's a lot more than I thought it would be. The video about Mount Rushmore was great, and the US Air Force Band is outstanding. The interpretative ranger was so well informed."

"I'll let him know you said that. Luis is a friend. I saw him when I was here yesterday." *Tell him the rest.* "I also ran into your brother and a reporter from Trent Media."

"Funny you should mention him. I saw my father and brother when I went to the men's room earlier. They were being interviewed by a woman with a cameraman recording everything."

"Did they see you?"

"My father saw me, but gave me the evil eye when he saw I was dressed in my cowboy clothes."

Her mad was back, full strength, but not at Shane. "Your father makes me so angry."

She cupped his chin to get him to face her. "Shane Walker, you listen to me. Soldiers are people who fight on the ground, from planes or from boats, in other countries or right here on American soil. They wear uniforms, complete or tattered, but it's what's inside that makes them a soldier. Honesty, courage, self-control, bravery, discipline, decency, conviction of purpose. I could go on and on."

She tapped the brim of his hat. "You may wear a cowboy hat, but it's what's inside of you that makes you a soldier."

"She's right, Shane. I told you I'd be proud to have you stand beside me when I go down to the stage," Mr. Berweiler said.

Shane nodded at the proud soldier sitting next to him.

*****

Shane leaned forward and buried his face in his hands. Nothing like being bombarded by patriotism in the form of words from well-meaning friends, two people he'd met only a couple of days ago. Everything Taylor had said made sense, a whole lot of sense. His father's and brother's sense of patriotism was warped, not his.

He had no more time to think. The lights dimmed, and the interpretative ranger announced Admiral Harwood Walker.

Stay or go.

Taylor stiffened beside him and covered the hand resting on his knee. "Stay or go."

The decision didn't come easy, but he drew on the courage inside him. "Thank you, Taylor, for making me see the other side. I'm going to stay, not for my father, but for what he stands for. He's a braggart and a blowhard, but he represents the Navy, our ancestors and all those men and women who gave their lives for our freedom."

Mr. Berweiler held out his hand. "I'm very proud of you, son."

"Thank you, sir. My father has never said that to me."

"Then he's a fool!"

His father spoke about their family in the military, all the way back to the Revolutionary War and supporting General George Washington and President Lincoln in the Civil War. Surprisingly, he included only a few details about his own career in the Navy. He did mention he had two sons in the Navy. When he mentioned Dane, by rank, a spotlight appeared on him sitting in the front row. He stood up and waved. The reporter was sitting right next to him.

"What a putz," Shane muttered and received a little poke in the ribs from Taylor.

"You're right," she agreed.

When the admiral was finished, the audience clapped, and the band played "Anchors Aweigh." The interpretative ranger walked onto the stage when the song ended.

"I hope you're enjoying this evening's program," Luis began. "Tonight, we have a special presentation. At this time, I'd like to invite Petty Officer Second Class Midori Sato to join me."

She walked proudly onto the stage. The spotlight made her summer white uniform appear whiter. She smiled and took the microphone from the ranger.

"Good evening. I'm here tonight representing the female soldiers in the United States Military. I'm sure a few of you might be wondering why I chose the Navy for my career. It's not because I love the water and will soon start training as a Navy fleet diver at the US Experimental Diving Unit in Panama City, Florida."

Shane leaned into Taylor and said quietly, "What a twist of fate. She's going where I was stationed."

Midori walked across the stage and met the interpretative ranger. He handed her a doll.

"I joined the Navy because of a diver who saved Sakura. This doll has been my best friend since I was three years old. When I was ten, I was visiting my grandparents in the Tohoku section of Japan when it was struck in 2011 by an earthquake and tsunami. During our rescue, Sakura was swept overboard. I was devastated. A Navy diver who had just saved two of his fellow divers from drowning, went back in the water to search for my doll."

Shane shook his head. *No, this can't be happening! She's here! The little girl from my nightmares with the doll! This twist of fate is about to become a life changer, not just for me, but for my father and brother!*

"I've been told he's here in the audience," the petty officer continued. "Would Lieutenant Shane Walker, US Navy, retired, please come down to the stage? I never got a chance to thank you."

Stunned when she said his name, not his brother's, Shane quickly looked at Taylor. Tears were running down her cheeks. She wasn't the least bit surprised. Twist of fate! She'd known. "What have you done?"

"Shane Walker, that little girl chose to be in the Navy because of you! It's time your father found out the truth! Go!"

"Go, son. Stand proud," Sergeant Berweiler encouraged, tugging on his arm.

"I'll deal with you later," he said to Taylor.

His legs felt like rubber as he made his way down the long steps to the stage. His father and brother were sitting in front-row seats on the aisle, and he had to pass them. His father put a hand to Shane's arm. "What's going on? Your brother saved the divers and the little girl's doll."

"It's time you got the story straight," was all he said and walked up the steps to the stage. The audience was clapping when he gave Midori a hug.

"I never got a chance to thank you. I joined the Navy because of your heroism. There's someone else who wants to thank you."

He looked up to see Benny Acosta walking in his direction in full dress Navy uniform. He held out a hand. "Thanks for saving my life. Also, for saving my life when we were in Naval Academy Prep School." His friend made sure he spoke directly into the microphone.

Luis walked out. "Ladies and gentlemen, Lieutenant Walker had no idea we were going to do this tonight. There are unsung heroes among us who should be recognized even if they only think they're doing what's right for their fellow man. At this time, we invite all military veterans and those on active duty to come down to the stage and be recognized. Please give your name and military service. Thank you for your service to our country. When we're done, please stand while taps is played, and we lower the American flag."

Shane was humbled, overcome by what had just taken place. Taylor! The bright lights prevented him from trying to find her among the crowd. Knowing her, she was probably still crying.

Benny held out his hand to Shane. "Congratulations, and it's about time you got the recognition you deserve."

"Thanks for coming. I really do appreciate it."

"It was all your girlfriend's doing."

"I don't have a girlfriend." *I wish I did.*

"Tell that to my mother, who wants to meet Taylor. She tracked me down via my parents' luncheonette. I'd like to stay around for the fireworks, but I've got to get back to base. Call me!"

While the men and women gathered on the stage, the US Air Force Band played the "Battle Hymn of the Republic."

Cameras had been focused on what had just taken place, and the reporter with his father and brother was talking into a small recorder. His father and brother had moved off to the side. From the way they had their heads together, it was obvious they were having a heated argument.

Shane felt a familiar presence when Sergeant Berweiler moved to stand next to him.

"Lieutenant Walker, it's an honor to stand next to you."

"Sergeant Berweiler, it's my honor to help you represent the men you served with, too."

He still couldn't believe all this was happening and looked toward the area where his father and brother had been standing, but they'd left. By rights, they should be standing onstage, too.

He couldn't imagine what his father was going through right now. Learning the truth his favored son was a coward and the one who raised his ire was a hero... No, he preferred to be an unsung hero.

Suddenly, the three men standing in front of Shane parted like the Red Sea. Bold as life, his father was standing in front of Shane. Behind his glasses, tears brimmed in his eyes. "I believe I owe you an apology. We need to talk, but not tonight."

Be kind. He came to you. "How about meeting with me at my trailer tomorrow? I'll text you the address of the campground."

"I'd like that." His father's back stiffened, and he bent his arm to give a military salute. "Son, I'm proud of you."

All his life, he'd yearned for this moment. This had to be a night of miracles. His father had actually said the five words he'd never expected to hear. He could barely get his next words out. *Courage.* "Thank you, Admiral. I mean, Dad. Where's Dane?"

"Nursing his ass from the kick he's been deserving for a long time. We'll talk more tomorrow."

The amphitheater full of spectators immediately went silent when the trumpeter got up onstage and played taps while the American flag was lowered. The band started playing "God Bless America," and two thousand voices rose in song.

The stage soon emptied, and Shane kept a firm hold on Sergeant Berweiler's arm as they slowly made their way up the steps to their seats. Taylor greeted him with a big smile. There was so much he wanted to say to her, but they'd no sooner sat down than a boom was followed by a sky full of fireworks behind Mount Rushmore. The band played the drum cannonade from Tchaikovsky's "1812 Overture" at the very end of the fireworks display.

Rather than try to leave along with the crush of two thousand people, they decided to wait until the crowd disbursed. A number of people thanked Shane for his service, but the Vietnam vet got more of the attention.

Shane turned to Taylor. "It was all you."

"I don't know what you mean," she returned, avoiding eye contact.

"Luis, your friend the interpretative ranger, Midori Sato, my buddy Benny, the unsung-hero speech. Taylor, it has your fingerprints all over it."

She relented with a deep sigh. "I've been sweating it out, not knowing if you were going to be happy or angry at the way I connived to get you here tonight."

"I was shocked, but I didn't have much time to think about what was happening."

"I guess I should tell you there's nothing wrong with Sergeant Berweiler's truck. He agreed to go along with my crazy plan."

He laughed out loud. "I've truly been had."

She put a hand to his cheek, but he removed it to place a kiss in her palm. "Like you said, unsung hero. I get it. I accept it. After all these years, I'm relieved my father knows the truth. As for my brother, I don't expect to hear from him anytime soon."

"I cried when I saw your father go up to you on the stage. What did he say?"

"To my utter surprise and shock, he apologized and will be coming to my trailer tomorrow. He wants to talk. Want to be there?"

"Absolutely not. You've been eating humble pie for a long time, but it's father-and-son be-honest time. He's seeing your brother in a whole new light. Is your father ready to accept he's helped make your brother the way he is? Maybe it's time your father grew up."

"There'll be lots of changes in the Walker family. Let's see what tomorrow brings."

He looked around and noted much of the crowd had thinned out. "I think we can leave now. Before I forget, thank you for making this happen. And I still don't think I'm a hero. I prefer being an *unsung hero*," he added with a wink.

Chapter 11

Nervous as a cat in a room full of rocking chairs had become her favorite saying. It continued to fit her even the day after the Fourth of July. She drank her third cup of coffee, looked out the window at Shane's trailer and wondered what was happening with his father. He'd arrived four hours ago.

When the trailer door opened, she ducked down so they wouldn't think she was spying. Shane and his father were taking Liberty for a walk. The admiral appeared ordinary in tailored slacks and a plain short-sleeved shirt. The other thing that was different—his stiff, military stance wasn't there. His shoulders were turned down in resolve, like he'd lost a battle. The sight pulled on her sympathetic side, and she felt sorry for him.

She sat down at her computer. The story idea was flowing at a quick pace. This book would have a time-travel twist to the story line. She could include her favorite ranger and a guest spot for Petty Officer Sato.

Before she got started on her story line, she'd mapped out her trip to Philadelphia. The 1,700-mile trip could be driven in twenty-five hours, but not in a forty-year-old bus. She was giving herself four days to make stops along the way to enjoy the sights.

She still needed to ask Shane if he'd like to accompany her. Her conscience had been quiet—she really needed to give it a name. Shane's acceptance of her deceit to get him to last night's program had been a stunner. No more manipulating. This decision would be all on his own.

She looked out the window again. *Taylor, it's only been ten minutes.* Two hours later, which had included eating a tuna fish sandwich, Taylor closed her computer. Except for some editing, she had a solid story. The images would be a challenge, but George, Lincoln, Theodore, and Thomas would look great.

The time-travel twist was an idea she'd definitely use again. Her mind was all abuzz with a great idea. A Navy diver could wake up on the *USS Bonhomme Richard*, commanded by John Paul Jones during the American Revolution, to help defeat the British warships *Serapis* and *Countess of Scarborough* off the eastern coast of England.

Taylor stopped and buried her face in her hands. Winnie jumped up and landed on top of the computer, knocking her hands down. She raised a leg and started licking her paw. "When I'm like this, I get out of control. I just told myself I'd no longer manipulate Shane, and now I want to write him into a book."

She ran her hand over the top of the cat's head. "Time to start battening down the hatches and putting everything away. The next adventure starts tomorrow morning at seven o'clock."

Whenever she had to give the interior an unlived-in look, it made her feel sad, but next stop, she'd take things out and make it feel homey. She'd just finished with the bathroom when there was a knock at her door. Shane!

She hurried to the front door, but was surprised to see Mr. Berweiler standing next to Shane. "This is a surprise. Come in." When neither one accepted her invitation, she became alarmed.

"Taylor, why don't you join us?" Shane's somber expression was worrisome.

The moment she stepped outside, he took her hand and guided her around to the front of the bus. *Not good.* "Shane, Mr. Berweiler, what's wrong?"

He squeezed her hand a little more. "When I took Liberty for a walk earlier, I noticed a small puddle of oil under Tillie. I called Mr. Berweiler, since he's well versed in engines, having worked on them for forty years. He was at the store and just got a chance to look at it."

Instinct had her getting down on her knees so she could look under beloved Tillie. Queasiness tightened her stomach, at the sight of a large black pool on the ground. She hung her head as tears streamed down her cheeks.

Tillie was dead. Her aunt's beloved bus was dead. The end of an era. She began to shake as the tears came harder.

A pair of strong hands gripped her shoulders to make her stand up. Shane's arms came around her, and she buried her face in his shoulder. He rocked her in place.

"I'm sorry, Taylor. If I thought there was a way to save your bus, I would," Mr. Berweiler said. "That's a combination of oil and transmission fluid. Tillie had a long, good run. I can't even put a Band-Aid on her."

She pulled away from Shane and wiped her face with the handkerchief he handed her. "The mechanic who has taken care of Tillie told me she was running on good luck."

She glanced once more at Tillie, and her heart broke a little more, if that was possible. Tillie was dead. "I have to think about what I'm going to do."

"Let's go inside Tillie and talk," Shane suggested. "Let me get Liberty. She'll never stop barking."

She nodded. *Talk? Talk about what? This part of my life is over.*

"Taylor, I'm sorry about Tillie," Mr. Berweiler said. "Thank you again for last night. You did the right thing for Shane and his family."

"Thank you, Mr. Berweiler." She gave the older gentleman a hug. "Please keep in touch."

Liberty must have sensed she was unhappy and jumped up to give her kisses. "Okay, girl. I didn't pack up all the doggy cookies yet."

Shane and Taylor stepped inside Tillie. Liberty made a beeline to the couch, and Winnie plopped right next to her. The sight chased away some of Taylor's unhappiness. They looked so cute together, then she remembered things had come to an end. Tillie would be going to a junkyard. *Oh, God! No!*

"You put everything away. It looks so empty in here." Shane braced a hip against the side of the counter.

~ 137 ~

"I'm leaving tomorrow morning." She sat on the couch next to Liberty and smoothed a hand over her head. "Or I was. I was planning to ask you if you'd like to visit Philadelphia with me."

"What are you going to do now?"

She shrugged a shoulder, staring down at the scarred linoleum in front of the sink. "I don't know. It's over. All my aunt's hard work. I won't be able to complete her dream." She expelled a deep sigh and hung her head. "It's over."

*****

Shane couldn't believe what he was hearing. The bus was dead, but not her life. His heart was breaking for her, but he needed to take a hard stand to make her understand all was not lost. She might not want to talk to him ever again, but she'd saved him, so now it was his turn to be the "hero" and save her.

He walked to a cabinet over the sink and slammed a door to get her attention. "This wood door is barely being held to the frame by rusted hinges. The print in the linoleum has practically disappeared. I'm sure the electric and plumbing are on their last legs. If you used the woodstove, you'd set the place on fire. The tailpipe is being held in place by duct tape. Tillie is old, and she needs to retire!"

She shoved up from the couch. "How dare you say that about my aunt's bus?"

"That's right—your aunt's bus!"

He moved to her bookshelf above the desk and pulled out one of Aunt Tillie's journals. He opened to the page that showed the places her aunt had planned to visit. To make a point, he jabbed a finger at the listing.

"You've been living your aunt's life, following her plan, writing the books she wanted to write. You've put aside what you wanted to do to follow your aunt's dream."

"How can you be so coldhearted? I loved my aunt and made her a promise. Tillie is dead!"

"Tillie the bus is dead, but not you!"

He pulled out a second journal and flipped it open to the first page that listed the title of a book and fanned the pages. *Murder in Paris*. "What about your dream? What about the foreign romantic suspense series Taylor Parish wants to write?"

He slammed the book closed. "Taylor, I'm disappointed in you. I never figured you as one to give up."

He didn't know what else to say to try to make her understand she had a life beyond *Adventures with Tillie*. He snapped his fingers, and Liberty jumped off the couch.

"If you want to talk, you know where to find me. I'm leaving tomorrow morning. Destination unknown."

His sneakers felt like they were filled with ballast as he walked away from Taylor. The tears running down her cheeks cut into him even more. He'd been hard on her, but it had been necessary. He walked out the door, but paused to put a hand to the side of Tillie. "Sorry, old girl. Didn't mean to insult you, but you really need to retire." He didn't expect an answer, but headed for his trailer, feeling he'd been kicked to the curb.

Liberty tugged on her leash, not wanting to leave Taylor and Winnie. "Leftover pizza for dinner. Then I have to pack up."

He'd just taken a bite of his reheated pizza when there was a knock at his door. "Taylor!"

His body couldn't take too many more shocks. Standing outside his door was his brother, Dane. "Are you lost?"

'No," he sheepishly replied. "Dad told me where to find you. Can I come in?"

Liberty growled when his brother stepped inside. "It's okay. He's friendly." *I hope.* Liberty jumped up on the couch, but gave Dane a challenging stare.

"This is small, but nice," Dane started, taking a seat at the kitchen table. He noticed the partially eaten piece of pizza. "Sorry to interrupt your dinner."

"Leftovers since I'm pulling out tomorrow." He removed a can of light beer from the refrigerator and set one in front of his brother.

"Thanks, I can use this." He took a long drink.

"What can I do for you?"

"You mean, is my ass still sore from our father's foot? I'll be able to sit down comfortably in a few months. He read me the riot act for my behavior and for taking credit for what you did." He drank a little more. "I owe you an apology many times over. Plain and simple, I've selfishly used your older-brother status as a protective shield. That's just an excuse, stealing your praise and pats on the back. You are and will always be a true hero."

Dane's humble apology made Shane feel uncomfortable, not used to his brother's sincerity. "I prefer being known as an unsung hero."

"When I return to Washington, I'll be putting in my retirement papers."

Shane's eyes opened wide in surprise. "Because of what happened last night?"

"Partially. It woke me up to cold, hard reality. I apologized to Petty Officer Sato. I like working with the media. Courtney Altman told me there would be a place for me at Trent Media in their department that covers the military. I'll be moving to New York."

"You always did like the spotlight," Shane teased his brother. "What does our father think of your plans?"

"Let's just say he's supportive of my decision." Dane looked around the trailer. "Is this your life now?"

Shane nodded toward Tillie. "That all depends. I'll know what I'm doing in the next few hours, hopefully. I'm dealing with a stubborn woman."

His brother laughed out loud when he read the name on the bus. "Tillie! That's where your girlfriend Taylor lives."

"For the time being. Tillie the bus is about to go gentle into that good night. She's got quite a travel history, but she's made her last trip."

"What is Taylor going to do with Tillie?"

"We haven't gotten that far." Shane pursed his lips. "Right now, she's not talking to me."

"Brotherly advice. Taylor is great and just what you need to be happy." Dane pulled out his phone and searched for a phone number. "I just texted you a name and number. A friend of mine is on the board of the Bus Museum of Transportation in Hershey, PA. Tillie would be a unique addition to their fleet."

"That sounds awesome. Tillie may not travel, but she could still be enjoyed by kids."

This camaraderie with his brother was a first, and Shane relaxed in his brother's company. Taylor had certainly worked miracles. When Liberty started beating her tail against the cushion, Shane surmised his stubborn "girlfriend" was at the door.

"I think you're life's decision has arrived." Dane stood up. "I'm out of here. Shane, I'm sorry. I know we're brothers, but I'd like to be friends."

"I'd like that." He shared a brotherly hug. "I'm sure you'll be hearing from my girlfriend." It felt so great saying that word.

He opened the door, and Taylor stepped back. The shocked expression on her face was worth the surprise at seeing Dane exit the trailer.

"Taylor, thanks for straightening out the Walker clan," Dane said. "Don't let my brother get away. Shane, see you around."

*****

~ 142 ~

She was going to do it again. Manipulate Shane. He'd been so right, making her recognize her dreams that she'd been avoiding for a few years. Dare she call him a hero for saving her? Yes, her hero had worked his way into her heart in a very short time.

When he'd left, she'd looked around Tillie and seen what he'd pointed out, and a whole lot more. Tillie was tired and deserved to retire. The thought that she'd go to a junkyard was gut-wrenching. *One step at a time.*

Would he go along with what she was about to propose? Liberty rushed over and offered her usual kisses. Keeping up this stiff pretense was hard. She really wanted to kiss him, but...

Before she sat down, he cleaned off the table and shoved everything in a garbage bag. "Have a seat. I'm out of food, but I can offer you water or a can of iced tea."

She folded her hands in her lap. "Water would be fine."

He sat in the opposite chair and drank from his bottle of water.

"You were right." She didn't choke on the words. "I've put aside everything I've wanted to do."

He reached a hand across the table and locked their fingers together. "I'm sorry for being so harsh and mean."

"No, you were the wakeup call I needed. I don't care if you don't like the word, but I'm going to say it. Shane, you are a hero, my hero. You saved me."

The smile on his face was slow coming, but it was there. "Tit for tat. You're my hero, too, for saving me."

"I've a proposal! A business arrangement."

"Should I write this down to make it a formal contract?" he teased.

She ignored his sarcasm. "As you're fully aware, I'm without transportation. If you don't have any travel plans, I'd like to hire you to chauffer me and Winnie to Philadelphia. Since Liberty is a new character in my books, she should be there so I can take photos of her on the scene. In return, I'll pay for the gas and campground fees and prepare all the meals."

"Other than the campground fees, I believe you made that same arrangement with me at this campground." Shifting into thinking mode, he tapped his bottom lip. "Your proposal sounds fair, but I've a couple of stipulations."

"I'm almost afraid to ask, but tell me."

"One, while we're traveling, you'll work on your foreign espionage series."

"I agree!"

"Two, you will consider letting Tillie become part of the Bus Museum of Transportation in Hershey."

"What? Are you kidding me?" Tears of happiness dribbled from her eyes, and she sniffed back the rest. "That would be so awesome, and she wouldn't have to go to a junkyard! The kids would be able to visit her, too!"

"Dane gave me the information. We can make a phone call tomorrow. We'll have to delay our departure a day or so, since we've got to move your personal belongings into my trailer."

"That's all your stipulations?"

"Nope, I have one more. Would you consider becoming my girlfriend and seeing where this new 'arrangement' take us?"

She tapped on her bottom lip, mimicking him, before getting up from her chair and making herself comfortable on his lap before kissing him. "Gladly, my unsung hero!"

Epilogue

"Close your eyes."

Taylor raised a brow at her husband and set aside the napkins she'd been folding. "As long as you don't let me walk into something. You've been acting strange all morning."

"Trust me."

"We'd better make this quick. Your father and brother are coming for the weekend, and I have to go in the house and finish making the salads for our barbecue."

"If they're early, Liberty and Winnie can entertain them."

Of course she trusted the man she loved with all her heart. In the last year, all her dreams had come true, even if she'd had to manipulate him a little more. He'd reluctantly become the naval hero in her latest espionage series. The *Adventures with Tillie* books had taken a back seat during the months school was in session. Living in Pensacola, Florida, she'd found there were a lot of places to visit when school let out. In a few weeks, she'd be visiting Luis at the Castillo de San Marcos National Monument in St. Augustine.

Shane had found his calling in restoring and refinishing school buses, by order only. He'd completed two, with three others under contract. He'd had to hire three workers. When his Blue Angels buddies weren't flying, they were frequent visitors and liked to work on the buses.

Two metal Morton buildings were on their twenty-acre property, so he didn't have far to travel to get to work. He was also giving diving lessons to children at the local diving school.

She heard the side door open, and the coolness of the interior of the metal building swept her cheeks.

"I'll count to three and then open your eyes. One, two, three. Open. Happy birthday!"

The tears started before she could say a word. "Oh, Shane!"

In front of her was something she'd never thought to see again. A mint-green school bus with the hand-painted cartoon on the side of a yellow-and-green-striped school bus being driven by a redheaded woman wearing a WWII leather flying helmet and oversize goggles. Her co-pilot was a striped Toyger cat wearing the same hat and goggles. The logo had been updated to include Liberty wearing WWII goggles. Adventures with Tillie II.

With the giddiness of a child, he grabbed her hand to draw her closer. "Do you know how hard it's been to keep you from coming out here? She's got solar panels on the roof so we can go boondock camping." He pulled a remote from his pocket, and the door slid open.

She stepped inside, not knowing where to look first. He'd duplicated the interior of the original Tillie as much as possible, right down to the woodstove.

"Shane, I'm practically speechless. When we visited Tillie at the museum in Hershey, I said my goodbyes, but I knew she'd never be forgotten. The director said they've drawn so many more visitors since featuring Tillie, especially children."

"I was pretty mean to you that day when I said Tillie needed to retire. Nothing said there couldn't be an Adventures with Tillie II. There's one thing this bus has that wasn't in the original one."

He drew her toward the back and opened a sliding door to display a smaller bedroom. His arm pulled her close so she could rest her head on his shoulder. "I love you, Taylor Walker. Think this is big enough for the next generation?"

"I love you, too, Shane Walker. Thank you for my wonderful birthday gift. Do you think the world is ready for more Walkers?"

"I'm pretty sure it can handle two more heroes!"

The End

Author's Note

I hope you enjoyed Unsung Hero as much as I loved writing the book. I visited Mt. Rushmore and the Chief Crazy Horse memorials. I hope someday you'll be able to visit these historic monuments, too.

To all of you who served or had a loved one who served our country, thank you. I'd also like to thank Luis Cabrera, Interpretative Park Ranger, for his invaluable assistance.

Want to find out more about my books and what's coming? Be sure to sign up for my newsletter, via my website. My stories are fun, sexy, romances that will make you laugh, cry, and fall in love.

Website: http://www.judykentrus.com
Facebook: https://www.facebook.com/judykentrusauthor/
Twitter: https://twitter.com/JudyKentrus
Instagram: https://www.instagram.com/judykentrus/?hl=en
Bookbub: https://www.bookbub.com/profile/judy-kentrus
Pinterest https://www.pinterest.com/jkentrus/_saved/

Goodreads:
https://www.goodreads.com/author/dashboard?ref=nav_profile_authordash

Amazon Author Central:
https://author.amazon.com/claim/join?query=Judy+Kentrus

Other great reads by

JUDY KENTRUS

ELUSIVE OBSESSION

MAID TO ORDER

LAUREL HEIGHTS BOOKS

ARREST OF THE HEART

Book 1

WINNER TAKES ALL – (Part One)

Book 2

THE WEDDING GIFT – (Part Two)

Book 3

TEA IN TIME

Book 4

FROZEN HEARTS

Book 5
US PARK RANGER SERIES

A KISS AT SUNSET
Book 1

KISS OF FIRE
Book 2

A TIMELESS KISS
Book 3

HISTORICAL ROMANTIC SUSPENSE

Spirit of the Winds

BEACON POINTE BOOKS
Romantic Suspense

THE ASSOCIATION
Footlight Theater Series

EVERETT – Book 1

JACKSON – Book 2

MASON – Book 3

RYDER – Book 4

Uncharted Love
Beacon Pointe, Book 5

EDEN PRAIRIE SERIES

DANIELLE'S CHRISTMAS WISH
Plus
Danielle's Snowy Wish
Bonus Short Story
Book 1

WRONG TURN, RIGHT HEART
Book 2
A Valentine's Day Romance

A WITCH'S TALE
Book 3

ANOTHER NEW YEAR'S EVE
Book 4

TASTE OF SUMMER
Book 5

Made in the USA
Middletown, DE
05 May 2022